ALIEN GAME

CATHERINE DEXTER

A BEECH TREE PAPERBACK BOOK
NEW YORK

The Library of Congress has cataloged the Morrow Junior Books
edition of *Alien Game* as follows:
Dexter, Catherine.
Alien game/by Catherine Dexter. p. cm.
Summary: As the students at her school become increasingly caught up
in the annual game of Elimination, Zoe grows more and more convinced
that the new girl in her eighth-grade class is not what she seems.
ISBN 0-688-11332-X
[1. Extraterrestrial beings—Fiction. 2. Schools—Fiction. 3. Science
fiction.] I. Title.
PZ7.D5387Al 1995 [Fic]—dc20 94-33240 CIP AC

10 9 8 7 6 5 4 3 2 1
First Beech Tree Edition, 1997
ISBN 0-688-15290-2

FOR MY THREE BEST READERS—
AMANDA, EMILY, AND ANNA

CHAPTER ONE

It found me, I'm pretty sure, completely by accident, a matter of pure chance. It could have been anyone in my school, anywhere in town, with a window open that night. Like with vampires—don't you have to invite them in?—this "being," which could cross space and time, had to look for an open window. And mine was the one it found.

It was a spring night, a school night, and I was up in my room, talking on the phone. I love it when spring is at its very beginning, when a warm afternoon comes out of nowhere, and everybody digs out a pair of shorts from their winter storage bags, and the ground smells so fresh, everything is new and yellow-green and sharp.

Anyway, I was trying to get off the phone. My

friend Amy talks a lot. She strings out every conversation so long that once my mother threatened to set the kitchen timer the next time she called. (That's so like my mother.) I was flipping through a new clothes catalog while I listened.

"Elimination starts this Friday," Amy said. "Are you going to let yourself get caught right away?"

"I don't know." I stopped at a photograph of a model on a dude ranch in Wyoming. She was perfectly thin and tall, and she was wearing a short denim skirt and a twenty-dollar T-shirt in a color called Tomato. (It also came in Storm and Algae.)

"Me either," Amy was saying. "All that screaming and running drives me crazy. It was funny, though, last year—remember Mr. Crawford? Claire got his name, and she started to run after him, and he ran—he actually *ran*—all the way to the library. It was so cute!"

"Mr. Crawford is pretty cute, especially for a math teacher. Listen, I've got to hang up. My mom's getting mad." That wasn't true, but soon it would be. "Bye, Amy." I hung up on her: rude but necessary. Then I looked at myself in the mirror. No sleek, long bones here, sorry to say. Just an ordinary, slightly plump face, brown eyes, and brown hair that's way too curly and has a life of its own. I bent over and brushed my hair upside-down ten times, then I stood up and looked again. Sometimes I do this just to see what's the worst my hair can do. I can brush up a globe of brown frizz that stands out in all directions—it's like living under a giant dandelion. Then I brushed my hair back down and sucked in my cheeks and turned at an angle to the mirror, trying to see what I would look like if I had "prominent" cheekbones.

I leaned close to the mirror and tried singing: "Ooh-ooh baby I'll be yours forevah/Just as long as yew keep pullin' my levah/Ooh-ooh baby we'll always be togethah—" My voice cracked on the last note. I'd started too high. The song was from a tape my other best friend, Rachel, had lent me. Rachel has two older brothers, Jordan and Tim, who have started giving her their old tapes and things now that she's in eighth grade. They've decided she's not a brat anymore and it's time to get her ready for high school. I wish they'd get me ready, too. Actually, Jordan scares me a little—he plays hockey and he's going to college next year. But Tim and I have always gotten along. He's fifteen and, like me, not much of an athlete.

I started singing again, lower: "Ooh-ooh baby I'll be yours forevah/Just as long as—" I stopped. Someone was there, in the dark, outside the house; I could feel it. I swallowed, and I heard my mouth make a dry, sticking sound. I held myself absolutely still, then stepped over to the window and looked down to the ground. I reached across my desk and turned out the light. I couldn't make out any unusual shadows or humps in the yard below. The breeze was soft, and a bird cooed, and something rustled in the trees. A car went up our street, its headlights poking slow cones of light through the dark. The only thing I could make out in the yard was a swarm of fireflies, a patch of winking, blinking lights, brilliant greenish yellow. No shapes moved in the dark, no stealthy footfalls. There was nothing to be afraid of. Besides, my parents were home. I knew they were right downstairs. I could picture them sitting on the sofa, watching the evening news on TV. As I thought of it, though, they began to seem awfully far away, like little figures propped in a dollhouse.

Of course there was nothing to be afraid of.

"Whew," I said, to make sure I could still say something. The word hung there like a cartoon balloon.

The real reason I wanted to get off the phone was so I could watch TV. Tuesday night is a heavy homework night, but I had already done everything—French, science, math—so I would have plenty of time for *Rescue 911*. I wanted to be able to sit there and enjoy it without a lot of stuff hanging over my head. It's one of my favorite programs, and just the other day Mr. O'Hara, my homeroom teacher, told me it was one of his favorites, too.

I looked around my room and decided I'd pick up when I was more in the mood. Towels and dirty clothes were in heaps on the floor, but that would take only thirty seconds to sort out; there were some empty cans of diet soda and scattered gum wrappers and clothes and crumpled-up shopping bags and tubes of hair gel and a purple nylon scrunchy and a glass with something incredible, probably organic, stuck all around the inside. I picked up the scrunchy—I'd been looking for it for over a week—and stuck it in my top drawer and went downstairs.

Actually, my parents weren't sitting on the sofa watching the news; they were in the kitchen having an argument, or anyway my mother was having an argument and my father was absorbing it. My mother is pretty moody, and my father mostly puts up with it and doesn't fight back. He says he likes to have peace in the household. Right now he was reading the newspaper and puffing on his pipe in silence while my mother complained about her sister, my aunt Diana. Zap, Mom swept a sponge the length of the kitchen counter, catching crumbs with her free hand and flinging them into the sink. "That's her problem," she was saying. "She's always had all that money; she doesn't know what trouble really is!" My father rustled the pages of the newspaper, which passed for a gesture of sympathy.

I tried to ease past the kitchen door.

"Are you finally off the phone?" my mother asked. "One of these days that thing's going to start growing out of your ear!" My mother will sometimes say these weird things, but if I tell her they're weird, she doesn't laugh it off, the way some people's mothers would. She gets her feelings hurt.

"I can't help it if Amy calls all the time," I said. "Why have a phone if you just want it to sit there?"

The phone rang.

"It doesn't just sit there," said my mother triumphantly. She reached to answer it. "Oh Francie. Hello."

"See, it isn't for me!" I said with a cackle. I went on down the hall into the living room and turned on the television set. I love *Rescue 911* because the stories are real, and they always come out all right. I can picture myself riding in the emergency vehicle, jumping out with my medical equipment, kneeling over the inert body, and expertly retrieving the life that has dwindled to a thread.

Other "real-life" programs get too scary. It's terrible, the things that people really do: Teenagers get shot on the street; mothers kill their daughters. A man took a woman for a ride on a sailboat, and two days later her body was found in a fisherman's net. Anything can happen. For instance, I thought, someone could have been in our yard just now.

I put that out of my mind. Tonight on *Rescue* a canoeist nearly drowned in a swollen river, but he was pulled out and suffered no brain damage; a boy got his tongue stuck to the wall of a freezer, and his baby sister dialed the telephone for help.

When the program was over, I went back upstairs to pick out my clothes for the next day. I called down good night to my parents, pulled a huge T-shirt over my head, and went to the bathroom to brush my teeth. I made a face at myself in the mirror, tried for the cheekbones again, gave up, and went back to my room. I closed the door, picked up the clothes catalog, and hopped into bed with it. But just as I had gotten all comfy under the sheet, I remembered again: On Friday they were going to start that silly game. I wished Amy hadn't mentioned it. It's called Elimination. You "kill," or "eliminate," people by running around and tagging them, and this goes on for a week. Everyone gets hysterical. The kids are the ones who insist that we play every year. The teachers don't care for it much. Supposedly the purpose is to get to know each other, but it's really just an excuse to run wild and grab people. People trick their friends; teachers pretend to give you safety holds, but really they're waiting to catch you off your guard; people jump out of the bathroom stalls at you. Last year my friends and I let ourselves get caught on the first day, just to get it over with. Lucky Mr. O'Hara—teachers can decide not to play, and no one cares or tells them they're taking it too seriously.

I couldn't get the little niggle of worry to go away, so I let the catalog fall to the floor and turned off my light. This is a moment that always makes me feel a little bit panicky, though that sounds babyish, because everything is uniformly black, whether I open my eyes or close them. As I lay there that night, waiting and feeling the dark press against my face, I suddenly knew for certain that someone had been in the yard.

CHAPTER TWO

When I went down for breakfast in the morning, my mother was standing by the sink, pressing her bathrobe to her waist with one arm and holding a cup of coffee to her lips like an emergency drink. She often looks this way in the morning, as if she has just been through something. I poured myself a glass of orange juice and put a slice of bread into the toaster.

"You know what? I thought someone was in the yard last night," I said.

"You what?" Mom moved away from the sink. Her face was still a little crushed from sleep.

"I thought someone was out there. Maybe spying on us, I don't know."

"Did you see someone?"

"It was more that I had this feeling. I looked out, but there wasn't anything. All I actually saw was a bunch of fireflies."

"Fireflies? At this time of year?"

"Don't ask me. I'm not Mother Nature. I'm going to look in the police report in the paper, see if there's anything about backyard prowlers."

"This has always been a safe neighborhood," my mother said.

"What would you do if there was someone?" I couldn't picture Mom running outside in her bathrobe to shoo away a prowler, or my dad, slow and methodical, lighting his pipe and taking a final sip of coffee before stepping out onto the back steps to have a cautious look.

"Why, call the police," said my mother. "You could call them yourself, if you ever need to."

My toast popped. I spread some margarine on it, then strawberry jam. I checked the clock. "Oh no! Where's Dad? Is he still in the shower? I've got a vocabulary quiz first period!"

My father is always the last person up in the morning, and he's maddeningly slow. He teaches at a law school, and he says if he's late, they'll wait. He makes two or three trips back and forth between the car and the house, carrying first his briefcases and books, then a mug of coffee; finally he goes back for his tweed hat.

"Dad!" I screamed up the stairs. "Hurry up!" I took a carton of yogurt out of the refrigerator and tossed it into my book bag for lunch.

As I went out the back door, I saw my mother go over to the stack of old newspapers and pull out a copy of the *North Point Gazette*. It has a whole column every week devoted to local crime.

No matter how rushed and frenetic I feel getting out the door, things always improve on the way to school—once we're moving through the flow of traffic, waiting at red lights, listening to the radio. My dad tunes in a classical-music station, and that seems okay, too, especially since it's so early. We don't talk much; we just think our own thoughts. This morning I tried to mention last night casually, as if it was no big deal.

"Dad, what would you say if I told you someone was prowling around the yard last night?"

He looked over at me as if he had suddenly woken up. He cleared his throat. "You mean after you went to bed? Did you see someone?"

"Not exactly, but I almost did. I had a really creepy feeling. Maybe I heard something."

"You should have come down and told us right away. But it's very unlikely that anyone would try to break in, especially when we're right there at home. You might have heard a raccoon knock over a garbage can. Not to worry."

"I didn't hear anything like a garbage can."

"I'll check around the house when I get home tonight."

We pulled up to the curb. "Bye!" I said, and jumped out and headed down the path. I love walking past the grassy slopes in the morning, though my parents are always telling me they send me to Oak Hill for the teachers, not the landscaping. Oak Hill is a private school.

I passed Josh Perkins, a little boy I sometimes baby-sit for, and I gave him a tap on his baseball cap.

"Hey, Zoe!" Dan Fields ran past me on his way down the hill. I've always been friends with Dan, which is good, because I know that if he ever decides on a girlfriend, it won't be me. If anyone ever decides on me, it will probably be Norton Peabody.

Rachel and Amy were waiting for me by Rachel's locker. We always meet there first thing in the morning, because Rachel's locker is the closest to the girls' bathroom.

"Can't use the girls' room this morning," said Amy. "There's a sign on the door: Some pipe broke, so there's no water. Want to look in this?" She held out a box of eye shadow with a tiny rectangle of a mirror in the lid.

I took a quick glance at a sliver of myself and handed it along to Rachel. Rachel is tall—she's always been the tallest one in our grade, including the boys. She started out tall and kept on being tall. "Willowy," says my mother, "and beautiful. Now, *she* has beautiful bones," as if they were something she'd been smart enough to pick out for herself. Rachel has long, silky black hair that she can wear up or down.

Amy hovered nearby, her arms full of books. Amy's the shortest of us, and she has cute freckles and friendly blue eyes. She latches onto whatever I'm doing ("a natural follower," says my dad), and then I feel better about doing it, just because she's along.

Henry Semp swooped by Rachel, giving her hair a playful yank. "Ugh," said Rachel, wrinkling her nose. Boys do like her, including the cool guys like Henry. There isn't one that's as tall as she is, though. Rachel says she doesn't like boys; she only laughs and walks away. But I can tell she likes having them like her. And that's only a step away from going out, and the next thing you know, she'll be popular. *Popular!* Even the word sounds hollow, like something empty with a hard, bright shell. I can't imagine that I'll ever be popular, and neither will Amy, but Rachel is on the brink. If she does cross over, I wonder if she'll shed her dumpy old childhood friends.

Rachel was bent over, arranging something in the bottom of her locker, her hair streaming over the shoulders of her jacket—a boy's satin baseball jacket in an awful maroon color. It used to belong to her brother Jordan. She slipped off the jacket, hung it on a hook, and shook back her hair.

"Wait for me—I'll just be a minute," I said. I raced down to the end of the hall and around the corner to my locker. That's when I saw them coming. Miss Albrecht, the assistant director of Oak Hill, was bringing a new girl down the aisle of lockers. This girl was very tall and thin, and she had straight blond hair, so light it was almost silver—I've never seen hair that color in real life—and green eyes and not a zit in sight. She was wearing a short denim skirt, though it was pretty chilly out, and a red T-shirt. She could have stepped out of that catalog I had been reading last night. Rats, I thought to myself. I hate being jealous of people; it never gets you anywhere except in front of your own mirror, grinding your teeth at all your faults and shortcomings. But here it was again, the nasty little knot, the ounce of hot acid in the stomach.

A herd of kids trailed behind the girl, pretending to be on their way to class but taking their time so they could look her over.

"Thought you'd be right back." Rachel came up, with Amy scurrying behind, the faithful puppy.

Miss Albrecht stopped at my locker. She is small and delicate, with snowy white hair and a gentle voice that she never raises. "Why don't you introduce yourselves?" she said to the three of us. "This is Christina Blake. Maybe you remember her from third grade. She's come back to our school. She's going to join us in the eighth grade, even though it's late in the year."

The circle of kids fell silent.

Amy warmed up right away. "I remember you! You were in Miss Barrington's class, just like me. I'm Amy Johnson."

"My name's Rachel Flaherty."

"I'm Zoe Brook," I said.

"Hi." Christina Blake gave a shy little nod and shook back her blond hair. She swallowed but kept the smile on her face and tried to meet our eyes. Then she turned and opened the locker. A heap of stuff, including a pair of smelly sneakers, an Oak Hill sweatshirt, some empty packs of gum, and an old raincoat, fell out.

"Woops! Better get my extra things," I said. I had

had the end locker all year, and I had spread out into the empty ones beyond. Now I'd have to figure out a new place for my extra stuff, and I'd have to be nice to the new girl, too, because I'd probably see her every morning.

I stooped over, and as I was scooping everything up, my eye caught Christina's. A shiver shot through me, like an elevator sinking thirty floors. She knew me. And, though I had never seen her before, I knew her. Not only did she look exactly like the girl in the catalog, she *was* the girl. A hint of a mocking smile played across her face.

I crammed my extra stuff into the bottom of my own locker.

"We're playing Elimination this week," Miss Albrecht went on. "You can play, too, and get to know some new names and faces."

"You don't know anybody, but that's okay," said Dan Fields, who had edged in until he was standing practically on top of Christina. He kept shifting his books and jacket around as if he couldn't get comfortable. "We'll teach you. Just draw a card, then hang on to two people. You can hang on to me for practice. Dan Fields is the name." He held out his hand, and everybody laughed, including Christina. She was even taller than Dan, but she looked graceful anyhow.

"They'll tell you all about it," said Miss Albrecht, looking relieved that the introductions had gone well. She peered at her watch over her gold half glasses. "Two minutes till class starts. Zoe, will you take Christina with you? She's in Mr. O'Hara's homeroom."

The eighth grade splits into two classes for homeroom. It was just my luck, I thought, that the new girl would end up in mine. Mr. O'Hara is the best teacher I've ever had. Actually, I think that every year, but Mr. O'Hara is really special. I can go by his office whenever I feel like it and talk about anything. He takes kids seriously, which is why everyone likes him. He's been at Oak Hill for only a couple of years, but he's one of the most popular teachers.

Henry Semp tugged at Dan's arm, and Dan let himself be towed away.

I tried to think of something to say to Christina as we walked toward the classroom, but I was feeling shaky, because I knew something very odd was happening to me. I knew I had never met this girl before, no matter what they said about third grade. But I was stuck with this feeling of total familiarity, like one of those déjà vu things, only it didn't go away. "Want me to explain about the game?" I finally managed to say. She stiffened and gave me a smile that said she'd find out on her own.

"Zoe!" Here came Norton Peabody, who seemed to have popped out of a locker like an old sneaker. He fell in behind us and caught the heel of my shoe with his toe. "Woops, sorry."

"Hi, Nort," I said, stamping my foot back into my shoe. Norton didn't seem to notice the new girl, but that's typical. He can get really wrapped up in his projects.

"Guess what my uncle Arthur told me?" he said.

We were going in the classroom door, and I couldn't pay attention. "Mr. O'Hara," I said, "here's a new girl. Miss Albrecht says she's in our class."

I guess I wasn't overly gracious. Mr. O'Hara was leaning against his desk, reading a note, and I swear he nearly jumped out of his skin when he saw Christina. Maybe they hadn't told him a new student was coming. The note sailed to the floor, and he just stared at her intently, and then he got back into his teacherly shell.

"Good, fine, we're happy to have you!" He pointed to a desk in the back of the room. "Norton, you and Adam please move that desk up to the front. There's room there on the side." Desk legs scraped across the floor. Mr. O'Hara stooped down to pick up the note, and then he turned to Christina. "Let's see...Miss Albrecht says you are Christina Blake. Would you like to tell us a little about yourself?

Where you come from?" He sounded out of breath.

Christina's voice was soft, like a very young child's, which was annoying. We all had to pay total attention to hear her. "I've just moved here from Wyoming. My parent and I came in early this morning to see if there would be room for me. Miss Albrecht said I could visit today, and start for real tomorrow."

Mr. O'Hara had a restless look while she was talking, as if he had something he wanted to say but was holding himself back.

"Your parent?" he asked when she was done.

Christina looked bewildered.

"Like, your mother or your father?" Henry helped out.

"Yes," said Christina.

"Good," Mr. O'Hara said. "Welcome. Now before we start class, let's tell Christina about Elimination. I don't know if you played it when you were here before—that was before my time. It's a game, and the whole school is going to play it, starting Friday. Anyone?"

Lots of kids shuffled their feet under their desks and pushed their notebooks around.

"Claire? Tell Christina about the game. Then we've got to get to our vocabulary quiz."

Claire McIntyre rolled her eyes and giggled.

"Well. It's like this. All the kids in the school except for the really little ones write their names on these cards, and then they're all put into a big box."

"It's not always a box. Sometimes it's a basket," said Norton, who is exacting about details. This uncle Arthur of his is a scientist, so maybe that's where he gets it.

Claire gave him a look. "We have an assembly Friday, and everyone files by the box and picks out a card. If you draw your own name, you put it back. Otherwise, you keep it. Then Mr. Bonner gives the signal—he's the head of the school, you know—and he stands in the middle of the assembly hall and blows a whistle, and we all start. You try to catch whoever's on your card. If you don't know who it is, you get other people to tell you. And somebody is trying to kill you, too, so to be safe, you make sure you're hooked on to two other people. As long as you're in a string of at least three people, you can't be caught. Or eliminated."

"It's called Elimination. That's the name of the game," Norton interrupted.

"When you kill somebody, you scratch through their name on the card you have, and you keep that card, and you also get the card they're holding. Then you go after whoever *they* were after. And if they've already caught people, you get all those cards, too. And it goes on like that till everybody is eliminated except one person, and they have all the cards. Only usually we don't go to the end, because it takes too long. We stop at the end of a week, and whoever has the most cards is the winner."

"The winner gets twenty-five dollars," added Norton.

Christina's face was bright pink. "Do all of you play? What about the teachers?" she said. She turned around to face me. "You're going to, aren't you?"

"Gosh, I guess," I said.

"Everyone in the eighth grade plays," said Mr. O'Hara. "But not every teacher."

"Aw, Mr. O'Hara!" groaned Claire. "Are you going to cop out again?"

"We'll see," Mr. O'Hara said. "One other thing. The rules say that you can play only on school grounds and only between classes and at recess and lunch. *Not during class.* Now, books away, everyone, just a piece of paper on your desk, please. Christina, why don't you take this test along with everybody else? We won't count it."

The room quieted. Mr. O'Hara perched on the edge of his desk, his quiz paper in hand, and read off the first word. His voice sounded normal, but I hap-

pened to notice that his hand was shaking so muc
that he switched the pages to his other hand, an
that one shook like crazy, too.

"Dan's got a crush on her, doesn't he?" said Amy.

Amy and Rachel and I were sitting at a table i
the lunchroom. We had managed to be the first in
to the room and helped the lunch-duty teacher ope
the windows. Now all the rest of the upper grade
came stampeding in, and the noise was deafening
Christina walked in with Dan Fields and Henr
Semp. Other kids looked over their shoulders at th
new girl, even the Duckies, who were sitting by th
window, at the best table in the room.

The Duckies are a bunch of girls in my grad
who go shopping for new clothes every week. Am
and Rachel and I call them the Duckies becaus
whatever Elizabeth Duckworth does, the others fol
low like a line of baby ducks. The Duckies currentl
include Kiki Wilson and Tam Sloane and Claire
and, of course, Elizabeth. (Sometimes someone els
gets more or less invited to be a Duckie.) They'r
small and blond and quick, and what they decide i
cool *is* cool, for that month anyhow. But at Oak Hil
supposedly everyone is respected as an individual
and we all have to contribute to the community
Teachers talk in class about respect for the individ

ual, and they talk in assemblies about respect for the individual. Elizabeth Duckworth said in the locker room one day that she could hardly wait for next year, when she could go to a school where everyone didn't have to be nice to each other all the time. It won't be much of a change for you, will it? I nearly said. Nearly. Elizabeth would have repeated it to her friends, and then they'd all have stood together, looking over their shoulders at me, or whispered when they saw me coming and then all gone silent as I walked by.

Sometimes I still wish I had said it.

"Why couldn't I have been born blond?" said Amy. She turned her piece of cold pizza around so she could begin eating at the pointed end.

Christina, Dan, and Henry stood by the door, scanning the room for places to sit. Then Christina began threading her way toward our table. My heart gave an uncomfortable knock.

"Mind if I sit here?" she asked us.

"Fine," said Amy. Rachel and I gave each other a look.

Dan and Henry went over to sit at a table of boys.

Christina sat down next to me, put her book bag on the floor, and took out a carton of yogurt. As she was loosening the top, I noticed it was lemon yogurt, the same as I had brought, and it was even the same brand, Yo-Yo Yogurt. That was quite a coincidence, because my mother buys it at a farm stand; you can't get it in a regular supermarket.

There was an awkward moment when nobody could think of anything to say. Plastic spoons clicked; paper napkins rustled.

"It must be so hard having to move in the middle of school," said Amy finally.

"I'm used to it," said Christina. "This isn't the first time. When I was here before, we didn't stay the whole year."

"To tell you the truth, I can't remember you," said Rachel. "But I'm terrible about things like that."

Amy frowned, as if she suddenly thought maybe she couldn't remember Christina, either.

"Well, I have this funny feeling I've met you someplace before," I said. "Not in third grade, but somewhere else."

Christina shook her head and said in a silky voice, "How could that be?" Her eyes looked into mine, and there was nothing friendly in them.

"What was your old school like?" Amy chattered on. "Out there in Wyoming, did you ride horses?"

"Do what?"

"Ride horses. You know, the Wild West and all. Did you live on a ranch?"

Christina hesitated. "I wasn't there very long, either," she said, which wasn't much of an answer.

"What was your other school like?" Amy kept on. "Was it bigger or smaller than this?"

"About the same."

"Our school is small, so we can all get plenty of attention." Amy rolled her eyes. "Anyway, I hope you like Elimination. They like it if we all play, but you don't have to if you don't want to. The older kids don't care that much about it. But everybody plays anyhow."

"Last year we let ourselves get caught right away, just to get it over with," I said.

"Really?" said Christina. "I'd never do that. I think if you play a game, you have to play to win. I always try to win. You can't just back out."

"Wait till you try it," I said with an uneasy laugh.

"I already have," she snapped. "Lots of schools play Elimination, only they call it by other names."

"Well," I said. I could feel my cheeks turn flaming red. I wondered why she hadn't said something about that before.

There was an uncomfortable silence.

"We only get twenty minutes for lunch. You better hurry up," said Amy.

Christina looked down at her untouched yogurt. "Maybe later. I'm not that hungry." She pressed the

lid back on the yogurt container and pulled a piece
of paper from her pocket. "I have to figure out where
I'm going next."

Amy looked over her shoulder. "Sports. I've got
that, too. Just as well you didn't eat a big lunch. I bet
you don't remember where the gym is. Come on, I'll
show you." Amy crushed the papers from her lunch
into a ball and scraped back her chair. "See you guys
later," she said, and she led Christina away.

"Look," said Rachel. The Duckies had all turned
around in their chairs to watch Christina leave the
lunchroom. The Duckies hardly ever turn around for
anyone.

"There's something weird about her," I said.

"You think so?" said Rachel.

At the end of school, I decided to stop by Mr.
O'Hara's office. I noticed that Christina's locker was
shut, and I was hoping she'd already left. I was feeling grouchy—though I didn't like myself much for
it—because she was attracting so much attention
and because I felt a little bit afraid of her, and
couldn't shake it off. I sure didn't feel like being
friendly to her. I went on down to Mr. O'Hara's office.

"Hi." I looked around the edge of his door.

"What's up?" Mr. O'Hara is tall and lanky. He has pale freckles and reddish hair that sticks up even after he presses it down with his hand. He is slow-moving and soft-spoken, and there is something sad about him. The reason everyone likes him is he listens to what kids say. Once I was telling him about how my mother gets mad and my dad just goes along with her, and he didn't joke about it as if it was a cartoon, and he didn't say, Oh, I'm sure they love you very much, blah, blah, blah. He just made these comments about how it's rough on family life if someone is always mad, and how did it make me feel, and things like that.

His office is incredibly neat—there's nothing lying around on the top of his desk, no funny mugs or dusty trinkets or collection of family photos. He has one photograph, though; I saw it by accident in the bottom drawer of his desk one day when he was looking for a manila envelope. It was of a girl who looked around thirteen or fourteen. I never asked him who it was; he's not the sort of person who lets you pry into his business. No one knows if he has a family. He's never mentioned one, and we all pretty much concluded that something awful had happened, a terrible divorce or something. He seems too nice not to have some relative somewhere.

"I just wanted to ask you something," I said. But before I could say what it was, Christina popped into the doorway.

"Hi!" She gave Mr. O'Hara a maximum smile. "Do you suppose I could borrow a book for the homework?"

"Didn't I give you one?" Mr. O'Hara went over to his bookshelf and pulled out a paperback of the novel we were reading in class. I could feel my heart suddenly *thud* and my mouth went dry. It was so stupid, because what was there to be afraid of?

"Thanks." Christina shoved the book into her backpack. I wished I had X-ray vision, because I could have sworn she already had a copy with her. "It's so great here," she said, spewing out friendliness like shaving cream at Halloween.

"It's great that you think it's great," I stammered, sounding a little thick.

"I was wondering...they don't ever change the day when they start the game, do they?"

"Not since I've been here," said Mr. O'Hara.

"Once they decide, they keep it," I said.

"Well, didn't mean to barge in. I didn't think you'd mind," she said to Mr. O'Hara.

"Anytime. I always like to see my students," said Mr. O'Hara.

She gave me a kind of afterthought smile that said, now I'm one of his students, too, and waved good-bye. I could see a couple of kids follow her as she walked up the hall toward the front door.

I turned to Mr. O'Hara. "Do you know her from somewhere else? You looked so surprised when you saw her this morning. Not that it's any of my business."

Mr. O'Hara didn't say anything at first. He tilted back on the rear legs of his chair, which he never lets anybody do in class, and put his hands behind his head.

"She says she was here in third grade, but we can't remember her. So..." I shrugged my shoulders. "Just wondering."

"I had a chat with Miss Albrecht this afternoon," said Mr. O'Hara, "and she said the front office couldn't locate Christina's old file because a pipe had burst in the records room. Christina brought her academic records with her from her last school, and Miss Albrecht decided to admit her now, since we have a space in the eighth grade."

"Was that it?" I said. Something still seemed odd.

"It's unusual for Oak Hill," Mr. O'Hara went on. He let his chair come down and got to his feet and began to put notebooks and file folders into his briefcase. "My old school was bigger than Oak Hil and there were always a few students coming in du ing the year."

"Anyway, so you didn't know her?"

"She reminded me of someone, that's all."

"She's so pretty, isn't she?" I was testing him ou hoping he would say he didn't think so.

"She's striking-looking, I'll say that."

"Want to know something? She kept seeming fa miliar to me, and I figured out that she looks exactl like a girl in this catalog I have—even the clothe Isn't that weird? Unless she's really her. I'll bring it i and show you. I've got it at home."

"You seem kind of fascinated with her."

"Well, she was sort of hanging around me, an she came to our lunch table, and she had exactly th same thing in her lunch as I did—this yogurt tha my mom buys at a farm stand. And if she just move here, how did she even know to bring a lunch at all:

"Hmm," said Mr. O'Hara. He was not being es pecially helpful.

"And you know what she said? She said they pla Elimination at lots of schools, and she's played it be fore." I began to fool with the straps on my back pack, stalling for time, because I could see that M O'Hara was ready to leave. "Have you ever heard c it anyplace else?"

"Actually, I have. The game has been around for a long time, going back a couple of generations, maybe much longer. It was very popular in the fifties."

"Did your old school play it?"

Mr. O'Hara had put everything into his briefcase and clicked the lock shut, but I didn't budge, I didn't take the hint, on purpose; I suddenly wanted to know more about Mr. O'Hara and games and his old school.

"As a matter of fact, we did," he said. The sentence came out in a rush, and I had this feeling that I was the first one he had ever told. Now he flicked off the overhead light, so I swung my backpack up and walked away.

"See you tomorrow, Mr. O'Hara!" I called to him, and gave him my usual wave, because he *is* my favorite teacher, and I didn't want him to think he wasn't.

CHAPTER THREE

"There's a new girl in our class," I told my mother when I got home. Dad drives me in the morning, but after school I walk home, if I'm feeling energetic, or take the bus.

"That's nice," said my mom. "Where's she from?"

"Some place out in Wyoming."

"I thought Oak Hill didn't take new students during the year."

"She says she used to go here, in third grade, so she isn't really new, so they can let her in. We can't remember her, though."

"Well, can't you take her word for it?" My mother's voice had a bright, irritated edge to it. That's how it starts when she's about to get mad. She gets into bad moods, and you don't always know

32

vhat you're in for when you come home.

"I guess," I said carefully. I opened the bread box
nd took out a loaf of bread. "I'm going to look for
ne of our old class pictures."

"We're out of jam," said my mother in a grating
oice. "And would you please take your laundry up
o your room? It's on the stairs, folded. I'm going to
ie down for a while."

When my mother is in a bad mood, the best
hing to do is keep out of the way, which is tricky
vhen I'm the only one home. My dad says we don't
inderstand why she gets this way and that we just
lave to be patient when it happens, until she gets
over it. Sometimes she'll stay mad for a couple of
lays. When my father gets home, he tries his best to
oothe her by fixing supper or doing the grocery
hopping. He will give a sigh and try to go along
vith whatever is bugging her. Sometimes I wish he
vould get mad back at her instead of always being
iice.

"I'm going up in a few minutes," I said. "I'm just
getting something to eat. I'm starving."

I turned my back and took a long time undoing
he twisty on the bread bag. Finally I heard her leave
he kitchen. I found the peanut butter jar. There was
till plenty in it, and it was the kind I like best—
:runchy and with salt. I made half a fat sandwich and

poured a glass of milk. I took a big bite and breathed a deep, clear breath. A moment later my mother's footsteps sounded, crossing the hall, coming toward the kitchen. But then she went off into the study and I heard newspapers rustling and a gentle thump. She must have settled down on the couch.

I finished the sandwich in three bites, gulped down the milk, picked up all my books, and headed upstairs. I scooped up the folded laundry on my way and piled it on my notebook. Maybe Mom would be all right after she rested. Sometimes that happened.

I closed my bedroom door, dumped everything on the bed, and went over to the mirror. Nothing new. Some days I do look better in the mirror, especially if I blur my eyes and try to even out my hair where it sticks up on one side. As I stared at myself in the mirror—blurred and unblurred—the feeling came over me that someone else was looking at my reflection along with me.

I stood there for a minute, because I knew no one else was in my room; I could see there was no one behind me. And furthermore, if somehow there was something, I didn't want to see it.

Then I made myself turn around. I think I twisted my neck or turned too fast, because for a second I thought I was seeing stars, a few little twinkles of ight in the corner of my eye. Of course there was nobody in my room but me. It looked a little disarranged—though it was hard to tell, given the way I usually keep it. My mom could have been up here collecting damp towels and emptying the wastebasket. She must have carried off that catalog, too, because I didn't see it on the dresser, where I'd left it.

I turned away from the mirror and picked up the phone and dialed Rachel's number. Rachel has flute lessons on Wednesday and Jordan is always at some sports practice, so Tim would probably answer, and he was the one I really wanted to talk to. For the sake of appearances, though, I had to ask for Rachel first.

"Not back from her music lesson," said Tim. He was chewing something crunchy that made a deafening noise in my ear.

"What are you eating?"

"Doritos."

"You're making me hungry."

"Sorry about that."

"Listen, can I ask you something? There's this new girl at school, and she says they play Elimination at lots of schools."

"And so?"

"And so I thought Oak Hill invented it. But then Mr. O'Hara said his old school played it."

"Sure, other places play it. I heard of somebody cousin who played it at college. It gets popular for while and then it sort of dies out."

"How does it die out?" I asked.

"I don't know; it just does."

"So how did it get to Oak Hill?"

"Sometime when Jordan was first there, that when they started playing it. He told me there wa this kid on student council who had the idea. H said it was like a chain letter—they had to play o they'd break the chain. So everyone got the teach ers to let them do it. I guess the kids told the teach ers that the student council should have some powe to do something real, and that made the teacher give in, even though they don't like it very much And it's been going ever since."

"I wonder where he got it, the first guy. Do yo know him?"

"No. I don't know what happened to him. H might have moved."

After I hung up I decided to give Norton a call. can always talk to him, and even though I get th feeling that he likes me, he doesn't seem to get hi feelings hurt if I don't like him back.

His mother answered the phone. She's an En glish teacher at the high school. Norton doesn' have a father, at least not on the premises; but he does have this uncle, his mother's brother, who likes to do stuff with him.

"Hi, Mrs. Peabody. This is Zoe. Is Norton there?" I felt like being completely polite, because she's really a nice lady.

Norton came on the phone. "Yo, Zo."

I rolled my eyes. "Norton," I said. "You want to know something I just found out?"

"Sure."

"They used to play Elimination at Mr. O'Hara's old school, but he never mentioned it."

"Well, that's a shocker." Norton can get sarcastic.

"That new girl said she's played it before, too."

"So? Listen, I'll tell *you* something. My uncle takes me sky watching sometimes—he has this telescope he sets up—and we're going to go tonight. He says something new was sighted in the sky last week, but it hasn't been seen since, and we're going to watch for it. If it isn't cloudy."

"How do you do that?"

"You pretty much sit there and watch. But you look in all different parts of the sky, and my uncle can find the constellations and all."

"It sounds a lot like fishing," I said.

"You have to go somewhere away from city lights and up high, if you can. We're going to go to Chickatawbut Hill."

"Won't you fall over the bodies?" I asked. High school kids drive their cars up Chickatawbut Hill at night to make out—everyone knows that. Chickatawbut Hill is this really small mountain out in the middle of Chester Hills, which is a big nature preserve a couple of miles south of our town. Sometimes the police go shoo the kids out; most of the time they don't bother. There's an abandoned school on top of the mountain, but you can't drive all the way up to it. There's a chain across the road at the bottom that's supposed to be easy to undo; then after you drive up to the top, supposedly you have to park and then climb over this high chain-link fence that *is* locked if you want to lie around on the grass and so forth. Some people say there's something up there and that no one knows what it is until they go see for themselves. I've also heard that the secret isn't that great. I don't know if I'd want to drive up there with a boyfriend anyhow. If I had a boyfriend.

"Uncle Arthur got permission to unlock the chain at the bottom of the road, so we can drive all the way in, and the gate up at the top, too," Norton said. "Want to come?"

This was beginning to sound more interesting. "What does he think you're going to find? A new planet?" Scientists do still discover new planets and moons, along with those black holes and other galaxies, and so on. "Maybe it'll get named for you! There's this thing on the radio sometimes where they advertise you can get a star named after you. The thing is, it costs around twenty-five or thirty dollars, and then what have you got?"

"You've got nothing and they've got your money," said Norton. "If you're going to name a star, just do it on your own."

"Mm." What I like about Norton is he's very practical. "So you're going tonight? Rats, my parents'll never let me go on a school night. How late do you think you'll be?"

"Probably late. We don't know. You can't set a time limit and do it right. We have to go by the sky. Listen, though, maybe we'll go again this weekend, so ask them now."

"You're so lucky your mom doesn't mind."

"Yeah—she's cool."

"My mom is not cool."

"Your dad's okay, though," Norton said, which kind of made my heart sink. I guess I'm always hoping someone will like my mother.

After I hung up, I went over to my closet and dragged out the box where I keep my school mementos. I started digging through it, down past the pieces of baby paper with big blue lines and words printed in six-year-old's handwriting; then some purple finger paintings with curled edges as crisp as dead leaves; then a thank-you note from my second-grade teacher for the shoe box of spice cookies. The third-grade class picture was under that. I pulled it out and took it over to the light. There we all were, in smaller versions but still recognizably ourselves, standing with Miss Barrington around the climbing structure in the playground. My hair was long then, and braided. Amy's little face was as round as a pumpkin. Rachel stood in the back row with a mischievous look, as if she had been caught pinching someone. Dan Fields had his hands jammed in the pockets of his baseball jacket and was grinning from the last row, and Norton stood beside him, a skeptical peanut.

I looked at each of the faces in turn. Christina Blake was not among them.

I was hungry again in half an hour, but I stayed up in my room until I'd finished my homework. Then I opened the door a crack. I could hear water being turned off and on in the kitchen, and there was the distant sound of someone talking on the radio. It sounded sort of lonely down there, with just the pots clinking and the radio. I imagined for a moment how it would be if my mother came upstairs and asked how my homework was going and what I would like for dessert tonight, and then said she'd fix it, whatever it was, and then announced that we were going shopping for clothes.

Something slammed, a door or a cabinet. Well, I could always go down and offer to help with dinner. That usually cheered her up.

Before I left the room, I tucked the class picture into a divider pocket in my notebook. Then I went downstairs and stood in the kitchen doorway. "How about if I set the table?" I said, making my voice sound perky. Supper did smell delicious: meatballs simmered in a big black frying pan. I took a pinch of grated cheese from a bowl on the counter.

"Why don't you see what you can find for a salad? I'm going upstairs to change." Mom's voice was clear and cheerful.

I rummaged around in the refrigerator, shook lettuce out of a plastic bag into the wooden salad bowl, and dropped in a couple of cherry tomatoes that were only a little bit wrinkled. I heard my father come in the front door.

"Anybody home?" he called.

"Hi, Dad."

"Something smells mighty fine." He stuck his head inquisitively into the kitchen, as if he'd never had a meal here before.

Mom came downstairs in jeans and a sweater.

"Zoe says there's a new girl at school," Mom said as we sat down to eat. "Not really new, though. She was in their third-grade class, and now she's back."

"That's nice," said my father.

"Maybe you should ask her over," said my mother.

"I'm not sure I need to," I said.

"Why not? Think of how it feels to be a new girl—even if you're an old girl."

"She looks like she can take care of herself," I said. "She's really gorgeous, you know. She looks exactly like one of the pictures in that Natalie O. catalog that came the other day. Did you throw it out? I thought I left it on my dresser."

"I thought you were done with it—it was all crumpled up."

Well, that was odd, because I knew I hadn't crumpled it up, and, while my mother can get into bad moods, she doesn't go through my room throwing away things that she knows I want.

After supper I offered to take out the trash and pack the old newspapers into grocery bags for the recycling truck. I saw the *North Point Gazette* on top of the heap of papers in the back hall, and I quickly leafed through it to the police column. It's always interesting, with all the incidents organized by crime: housebreaks, burglaries, arrests. I didn't see any category for Peeping Toms.

I lugged the bags of trash out to the garbage can, beside the garage. Light still lay along the western horizon, though it was dark by the porch, so I walked around to the backyard, which had a good view of the sunset. A line of low clouds was lit with gold. I looked straight up into the inky blue sky, wondering if I would recognize a new planet or celestial thing if I saw one. I love our backyard, though it's small and it's been years since I actually played in it. It still seems like my private territory.

Beside the dogwood tree is the park bench my father and I rescued once from a dump. When she found out where we got it, my mother said, "Ugh! What were you doing prowling around the dump?"

"Looking for a bench," I shot back. "We weren't *prowling*, Mom, gosh!" Dad and I worked for days to sand it down to bare wood and give it coats of glossy black paint.

And here was the spot among the apple trees where I saw the fireflies last night. I stood for a moment, remembering the pinpoints of light, pulsing, as bright as diamonds. What if the lights had not been fireflies but something else?

I sometimes like to tease myself with stories that *could* be true in the furthest stretches of imagination. What if there were other kinds of shapes in the yard right now, shapes I could almost see, but not prowlers, not Peeping Toms, not something I could call the police about? Every now and then there was a flock of UFO reports in the news. What if a pale blob stuck its tentacle out from behind the trash can right now? Or what if some huge silver saucer, glittering with thousands of lights, as big as a stadium, hovered overhead and freezing green rays shot out and I was paralyzed and then slowly drawn up into the arms of the mother ship—

I heard myself give a scream, and I dashed back into the house. I started to laugh, but I was shivering at the same time. My father was the only one in the kitchen. "I got spooked out there!" I said, and went off into a fit of giggles.

"You didn't see someone, did you?" my father asked sharply.

"No! Nobody was there. Nobody at all." I made myself stop laughing and went over to the kitchen window and peered out to make sure. But it was light in the kitchen and dark outside, so of course I couldn't see anything anyhow, even if there had been a hundred pale blobs creeping around the trash can. I almost wished a blob had been there. Then there would have been a solid reason why I felt so scared my teeth and knees were clinking around like ice cubes in a glass of tea.

I went to bed early that night. I woke up much later when I heard the phone ring. We sometimes get wrong numbers in the middle of the night, and I didn't want to get up to answer it. I didn't even want to turn over and open my eyes to see what time it was. I lay there with my head under the quilt, listening and counting the rings—four, and then part of one, and then the answering machine came on. My room was perfectly quiet after that.

CHAPTER FOUR

My mother noticed the answering machine blinking the next morning as I was sitting down with a bowl of cereal. "Guess we slept right through the phone last night," she said. She pushed the playback button and went on measuring coffee beans.

"Hi, Zoe." It was Norton's voice, and I could tell from his first words that he was upset. "I know it's too late to call and I'm sorry, but I was hoping you might still be awake, because I need to tell you something bad has happened to my uncle. So maybe I'll see you at school tomorrow, if I'm there. Bye."

"I heard the phone! If only I'd gotten up!" I said to my mother.

"Why don't you call him now?" she suggested.

Nobody answered when I dialed his number.

"Is there anybody else we can call?" I asked. "Who are they friends with?"

"I don't know offhand," said my mother. "We shouldn't just go calling around, anyway. That's how rumors get started." I didn't mention the sky-watching expedition, much less that I'd been invited to go along.

"There's nothing to do but wait till you see him," said my father as we rode to school. "I know it's hard to wait when you're afraid of bad news." He gave my hand a pat. "Have you got any change? Give me a ring at recess, even if you haven't found out anything. Okay?" He handed me some coins.

We stopped so I could get out at the top of the hill, and I saw a sleek black car with dark windows down by the front of the school. It looked almost like a limousine. "Wait a second—see that car down there? Can you take me to the front door? Just this once?"

Dad sighed and shifted into drive. He doesn't like getting stuck in the slow carpool line. He stopped behind the black car as its front door opened and Christina Blake slid out. I was expecting to see a uniformed driver behind the wheel, but the car pulled away too quickly to tell who was driving

it. It was almost as long as a limousine. A cluster o
kids watched it go. It sure beat the usual family mini
van.

"Talk to you later," I said, and jumped out of ou
car. I was several yards behind Christina, but I coul
see that she was wearing the same clothes as yester
day. Maybe she had a dozen of everything.
Christina passed Josh Perkins and his friends, and
they nudged each other when they saw her. One o
them looked up shyly and said, "Hi!" She gave then
a big grin and tilted her head, letting her hair swing
out like silk in the sun.

I could feel my own hair sticking to my scalp and
curling and frizzing out. My jeans were too tight,
and I noticed a damp place where toothpaste had
dribbled down onto the front of my T-shirt.
Christina was walking fast, light on her feet, and
felt like a shapeless blob trying to hurry behind her.
I tried to make myself not care, slow down. I didn'
want her to see me and start telling me how great i
was here.

"Hi, Josh," I said, a little too loudly, when
caught up to him.

"Zoe, hi!" He gave me a smile, and I felt better.

When I got to my locker, I didn't see Christina
anywhere. Maybe she'd already gone to homeroom

put my books on the top shelf of my locker, opened my notebook, and slid out the class picture from third grade. Amy came up behind me. "What's that?"

"It's us in the third grade. Listen, you haven't seen Norton, have you? Is he at school yet?"

"Haven't seen him."

"Something bad happened to his uncle last night."

"Oh no!" Immediately, Amy was on the verge of tears, and she didn't even know why.

"I want to find out what it is as soon as he gets here," I said.

"How come you brought that?" Amy pointed to the photo.

"Look at it. Christina Blake isn't in it."

"Maybe she was absent. One year I was absent, and every time my dad picked up the class picture, he would say, 'Now, where are *you*?' No matter how many times I told him."

"But there are twenty-two kids. That's the most there's ever supposed to be in a class."

"So what if she wasn't in it?"

"Then why did Miss Albrecht say she was?"

"Who cares?"

"I just don't think the school makes mistakes like

that!" I pressed my lips together. Sometimes Amy can be so dense. She began clearing her throat like mad. I turned around. Christina was standing behind me, twirling the combination lock on her locker.

"What's the picture?" Christina said, looking over my shoulder. I could smell a familiar fresh-soap scent about her, as if she'd just stepped out of a shower. She must use Pears soap, like my family does, I thought. Not that many people do.

"Third grade. I can't find you in it, though."

"Mm." She studied it.

Amy said, "It must have been taken after you left."

"That must have been what it was," Christina agreed.

I didn't say any more about it, but I put the picture back in my notebook.

"See you," Christina said, and drifted off down the hall.

The first thing I saw when I got to the classroom a few minutes later was a group of kids standing around Mr. O'Hara's desk. Christina was right in the center, talking to him. Probably she'd be going to see him every day after school, too. I glanced everywhere, but no Norton. I put my books on my desk nd then I went up and stood next to Christina to near what was going on. It sounds strange, but I couldn't stop staring at her arms and legs, they were o smooth—they didn't even look like regular skin. Then I realized why: She didn't have a single hair on hem, not even any fine, light hairs on her arms.

"It's the kids' thing entirely," Mr. O'Hara was saying. "The school decides how long it goes on, but hat's all. We have a limit of a week."

"How come you never play?" asked Claire.

"I wouldn't say never," replied Mr. O'Hara. He tood up and shook off his audience. "Could I have our homework, please?" As they all went back to heir seats, I saw Christina's eyes meet Mr. O'Hara's, nd some kind of a look passed between them.

"So *are* you going to play?" She repeated the question to Mr. O'Hara as she was sitting down. It vasn't the tone of voice you'd expect a brand-new tudent to use with her teacher.

Mr. O'Hara acted as if he hadn't heard her. "We need to take a minute and do our cards for the game," he said. He picked up a bundle of little cards from the corner of his desk and handed them to the person in he first row. They were index cards, cut in half. "Please take one and pass them along. Write your whole name on the card and pass it back to me."

"Should I do Norton's?" I asked. "He isn't her yet."

"Good idea," said Mr. O'Hara. "He wants to play I know that."

I took two cards when they came to me, wrot our names on with a blue ballpoint pen so they wouldn't get smudged if they got handled a lot, an passed them back up.

While we were scribbling, Mr. O'Hara was writing something, too.

"Are you doing one for yourself?" asked Kiki.

"Maybe, maybe not," said Mr. O'Hara.

When we'd all finished, Mr. O'Hara gathere the cards into a neat stack and put a rubber band around them. "I'll give these to Miss Albrecht," he said.

"When are we doing the drawing?" asked Adam

"At morning assembly tomorrow, as far as know," said Mr. O'Hara.

I kept watching for Norton all morning. He didn' come during English or math or recess. Meanwhile Christina was dazzling kids right and left. She wa even starting to work on the Duckies. I could se them watch her when she tried to answer a math problem, and you could just tell they were deciding whether she was cool or not, and if she was, how cool.

Norton came in halfway through science, while we were doing our sludge lab. That's the one where we use real chemical powders to identify what's in a test tube full of murky water; it's everyone's favorite. Norton handed a note to Miss Brigham and came over to my table. Miss Brigham lets us talk while we do our labs, as long as we're really working.

"What happened?" I said to Norton. "How's your uncle? Where is he?"

"In the hospital. My mom and I went to see him this morning. He's unconscious."

"What happened? Tell, Norton, come on!"

"Well, when we got up on Chickatawbut Hill, he got hit by something like a bolt of lightning. It burned up the telescope and knocked him ten feet through the air."

"Did you get hit, too?"

"No, I was off by the car, putting on a sweatshirt, lucky for me, and for him, too—if we'd both gotten struck, we'd have been up there for hours. He was moaning, but at least he was still breathing, so I ran all the way down the mountain and waved at a car on the highway. He stopped and had a car phone, so he called the police and then he drove up there with me."

By now the entire science class had stopped tinkering with the fluids and was dead silent, listening to every word.

"Let's take a few moments and hear Norton's story," said Miss Brigham, who knows what's important and what isn't.

"When we got back up there, we were afraid to go out in the open where he was, because lightning kept cracking out of the air, and we thought, you know, we could get zapped, too. There weren't any storm clouds; the weather was perfect. That's why we went up there. But these bolts started coming out of nowhere. He was lying down flat; he was way into the grass. So this man and I, we waited for a few minutes till we heard the ambulance, and it came up to the top, and a couple of the EMTs crawled on their stomachs all the way out to him. There was hardly any lightning left by then, but they got down as low as they could and dragged him across the field to the ambulance. And the police came, too, and they took me home."

"Well," said Miss Brigham after a moment. "I hope you'll have good news about him very soon."

"Thank you," said Norton.

Everybody turned back to their experiments. Norton gave me a worried look. "I never saw lightning that close up before," he said in a low voice. "It wasn't like regular lightning."

I happened to look up, or maybe something nudged me; way across the room, I saw Christina staring at Norton, and for the first time the smile was gone from her face.

Christina didn't come to our table at lunchtime, but Norton did. He slid into the empty chair beside me and put his lunch on the table, a wad in a brown paper bag, smelling of dill pickle and raw onions. Norton packs his own lunch, I'm pretty sure.

"Norton, what's in that? It reeks!" I said.

Norton pulled out a sandwich that was already falling from uncertain folds of waxed paper. "Salami and onions. Want a bite?"

"Uh...no, thank you." I popped the lid off my yogurt. Still, the salami smelled good, and Yo-Yo Yogurt seemed kind of insubstantial in comparison.

"I hope your uncle will be all right," said Amy.

"You must have been so scared," said Rachel.

"I was," said Norton. "The doctor told my mother they don't know much yet, but when he wakes up, then they can tell how he is."

"I wrote you a card for the game," I said.

He nodded, chewing on his sandwich.

"So what do you think of her?" asked Amy. We could see Christina standing by a boys' table on the other side of the room. "Do you think she's pretty?"

"No, I don't," said Norton. "I don't like her."

"Me either," I said.

Norton crunched a pickle in two, examined the second half, then popped it into his mouth along with the first. "She's older than she pretends to be," he said.

"You think so?" I asked.

Norton shrugged. "Older than eighth grade, anyhow."

Now Christina was dodging around chairs, laughing, playing a game of tag with Dan and Henry. They were trying to stay out of her reach.

"Isn't it amazing how she's fitting in?" Miss Grabill, who was on lunch duty, was standing right behind my chair, talking to Mr. Spencer, a fifth-grade teacher, also on lunch duty.

"I understand she's been here before. Eleanor Albrecht says she's not really new," said Mr. Spencer.

"She only *says* she's been here before," I said, turning around. "We think she's making it up."

Rachel poked me with her elbow.

"We do!" I said.

"Yes, well," said Miss Grabill.

"I'm sure Miss Albrecht knows," said Mr. Spencer.

"Oak Hill always makes new students feel welcome," Miss Grabill added loftily.

Now Kiki had stepped over to Christina and was whispering something to her. Christina followed her over to the Duckies' table, and they sat down together. I don't think a Duckie has ever sat next to me unless she had to, like at an assembly with assigned places.

The bell rang. "Going to help her find sports again?" I asked Amy sarcastically.

"There's nothing wrong with her except that she's too pretty," said Amy.

"Hey, I forgot I was going to call my dad," I said. "I'll see you guys later." My father probably wouldn't have cared if I waited till supper to tell him about Norton's uncle, but I somehow wanted to hear his voice. I went to get some change out of my locker. The second bell had rung by the time I got to it and opened it. I took out the coins I'd stacked in the corner. The pay phone was upstairs, across from the front office where Mrs. Webster, the school secretary, sat. Mrs. Webster was famous for remembering everything.

I pulled out my notebook, the one where I'd

tucked in the third-grade picture. I had the idea that I could ask Mrs. Webster about it. I took a quick look, just to make sure the picture was still there, and then I pulled it out all the way, because something was wrong—it had faded so much since morning that all the faces were nothing but blurs. I kept staring at it all the time I was calling Dad and telling him what had happened to Norton's uncle. I carried it around with me the rest of the day, but I didn't show it to anybody.

CHAPTER FIVE

That night at supper we were talking about Norton and his uncle, and my father mentioned an article he had seen in the science section of the newspaper. "Let me see if I can find it." He got up and rummaged through the stack of newspapers in the back hall. "Here we go." He pulled out a section and folded it back and brought it to the table. "'Last week university astronomers as well as several local amateurs reported having seen an unidentified bright object in the nighttime southern sky. The object was sighted twice, and was not visible steadily, but for only a few minutes on two different nights. Observers were unable to determine what it was. Anyone who sees the object is invited to note down time and location and notify the Whittemore Observatory at the university.' That must have been what he went out to look at."

"I wonder if he actually got a look through his telescope," I said. "Maybe he saw what it was before he got hit."

The special assembly was scheduled for 8:45 on Friday morning. Most Friday mornings people are a little off the wall anyhow, and today everyone was totally manic. Mr. O'Hara looked resigned to it. Norton came in late, but he looked a lot more cheerful than he had yesterday.

Our class walked down to the assembly hall. Miss Albrecht was standing in the center, holding a big canvas shopping bag in which she had put all the cards with our names written on them. The music teacher, Miss Graham, held up two fingers in the signal for quiet. Some of the kids stopped talking.

"We'll draw our cards now—line up by classes, please—but remember, nobody starts until Mr. Bonner blows his whistle!" Mr. Bonner nodded bleakly from the back of the room. A silver whistle, hanging on a leather string, gleamed against his tie. Everyone can tell he doesn't like these occasions when he has to be officially silly and hearty.

We started to file by Miss Albrecht by class. "All the Nelsons!" announced Miss Graham. "It's the Nelsons' turn!" The fourth graders in Miss Nelson's class lined up.

Miss Albrecht carried the bag over to Mr. Bonner. He drew a card and slipped it into his shirt pocket. She offered the bag to Mrs. Thompson, the school cook, who drew a card, chuckled, and tucked it into the belt of her white nylon dress. Even Mrs. Webster was there and drew a card.

The drawing didn't take long. A few cards fluttered to the floor, and kids tried to peek over each other's shoulders. Everyone got nervous and excited as more and more cards were drawn. Teachers drew cards with their classes. The eighth graders were the last to file by Miss Albrecht. I watched Christina being shepherded along by Dan Fields. She reached into the bag, took out a card, glanced at the name, then folded it in half. I was ahead of Amy, and Rachel was somewhere behind us. I looked away, sifted through the cards with my fingers, and chose one. As soon as I had taken my hand out and it was too late to stir the cards around and take another, I knew whose card I had drawn. I didn't even need to look at it.

Mr. O'Hara was at the end of the line of eighth graders. He shook his head when Miss Albrecht offered him the bag.

I searched out Rachel and Amy, and we linked

arms so we would be safe as the last cards were drawn. Finally there was only one card left: Miss Albrecht reached in and drew it out. Everybody cheered. Mr. Bonner came to the center of the hall and held up his hand for silence.

"The game of Elimination is about to begin. You've all discussed the rules in your classes. We will play for ten minutes before returning to our classrooms. Ten minutes only. Are you ready?" He didn't wait for the chorus of yesses, but blew a blast on the whistle. The room seethed as everybody screamed and grabbed each other's hands in a giant chain reaction. Mr. Bonner gallantly allowed Miss Albrecht and Mrs. Webster to latch onto his elbows.

Strings of kids built up like molecules, as triplets formed, and then seized hands with other kids.

Rachel and Amy and I inched to the edge of the assembly hall. Little children all around us were squealing. Several of them had been caught immediately and had had to surrender their cards practically before they'd read them. Christina Blake was in the center of a mixing bowl of fifth graders, with Dan Fields still holding one of her arms and Henry Semp fastened to the other. Dan was pointing out somebody, and Christina was nodding.

"Who've you got?" asked Amy. "Look at mine," she went on, without waiting for an answer. She unfolded the card she had already folded and refolded into a tiny square. "Michael Morris. Who's that?"

"He's a little kid. I know him. Sort of light hair and a lot of freckles," said Rachel. "I've got Mr. Bonner!"

"Oh no!" Amy and I said together. We looked over in Mr. Bonner's direction and saw him proceeding toward the assembly hall door, with Miss Albrecht and Mrs. Webster trailing at his sides.

"And guess who I've got." I turned over my card. But it wasn't the new girl after all. "Molly Frick." A seventh grader. We were in art class together during last period on Fridays.

"Look!" said Amy. "There goes Mr. Crawford."

Mr. Crawford, usually a solemn-looking teacher, went racing across the end of the room and out the door, a wicked grin on his face.

I looked around the room, and then I caught sight of Christina coming up behind Josh Perkins. He was standing just a little way from me, holding his card and looking between it and the kids swarming past him. Two of his classmates saw Christina coming toward him. They screamed and jumped up and down and pointed, but none of them was holding on to him, and when he half-turned to look over his shoulder, Christina tagged him. She bent down and gave him a big smile, as if to compensate. Then, as I watched, he did something strange and very un-Josh-like. He stood absolutely still for three or four seconds, looking right up into Christina's eyes. When he looked away, his mouth fell open and a little bubble of spit beaded on his bottom lip and strung down a gleaming strand to his shirt. Then he came to himself, said "Oh, shoot," and handed over his card and stuck his fists nonchalantly into his pockets, as if he didn't care at all.

"Who'd you have?" one of his buddies asked him.

"You're not supposed to tell," he said.

Christina looked like she was consulting with Dan and Henry about the card she'd taken from Josh. The three of them had linked arms, and Dan gestured with his elbow toward another knot of kids. They all began to scream and clutch hands when they saw the trio of bigger kids move toward them, but they didn't try to run away; they just stood there and screamed.

"Don't let go!" shrieked the little girl at the end of the line.

"I don't think he's here," said Henry, too loudly.

"He's trying to fool you!" cried a child in the middle.

They screamed again and laughed and held on tight.

Henry made a show of letting Christina and Dan

see his card. They whispered together, pretended to lose interest, and moved away. The little ones looked at each other and giggled with relief, thinking they had held off the invader. But it was hard for them to coordinate holding on to each other and holding on to their cards as well. Hands came apart easily and elbows got unlinked; somebody had to sneeze, and that wrecked the whole line. Christina was there. She put her hand on a little girl's shoulder. "Got you," she said.

"Oh!" the little girl said in a hiccupy chirp. She looked up at Christina and kept looking at her for several seconds, as if she was dazzled. Then she laughed and handed over her card. "Drat!" she said.

"Did you see that?" I asked Amy.

"See what? Oh, God! Claire's trying to get Fitz!"

Amy and Rachel were watching Claire, who undoubtedly wouldn't have bothered to play if she'd drawn anyone else's card. But if you drew a cool person's card, you usually went after them. I saw Christina move on to a third person, a teacher this time, Miss Grabill.

"Aren't you quick!" Miss Grabill said, and she, too, smiled at Christina and looked dazed. Then she handed over the card she was holding.

"Hey, what's she doing? Hypnotizing everybody?" I said. No one paid any attention.

"She got him!" Amy screamed. Claire had cornered Fitz, and he raised his hands like a movie cowboy. Claire put her hand on his chest, looking around to make sure her friends saw her, and then held out her palm for Fitz's card.

I nudged Rachel and pointed toward Christina. Coached by Dan and Henry, she stepped up behind Mrs. Thompson and tapped her on the shoulder.

"You didn't give me a chance!" Mrs. Thompson laughed good-naturedly and grinned at Christina and went on grinning while her eyes focused on something in Christina's face.

"Did you see that?" I said.

"See what?" said Rachel. "All I see is she's really into playing." She looked down at her card and sighed. "Well, shall we play for a while or let go?"

"Play!" I said. I gripped their hands so tightly, Amy yelped. "Don't anybody let yourself get caught."

Christina turned then, and I saw her looking at the three of us. "Let's go," I said, and began to yank Rachel and Amy across the assembly hall.

"What's got into you?" Amy said.

All strung together, we dodged our way to a side door as the ten-minute bell rang. We headed for the eighth-grade classrooms in the far wing of the building. The Duckies passed us in the hallway—fastened together, naturally.

"Hurry up," said Kiki, looking over her shoulder at me, and they sped away up the corridor.

We tumbled into Mr. O'Hara's classroom just as the bell rang again. Rachel gave a little whoop and raced away to her own class. More eighth graders jostled through the doorway.

"She's already caught on!" Dan Fields announced to the class. "I showed her who her first card was, and she got him right off. Then I showed her the next name, this second-grade girl, and she got her, and some other ones, too, and a teacher. And Mrs. Thompson."

"No wonder, if you're helping her," said Claire.

Christina held up her handful of cards and looked modest and embarrassed at the same time, as if she couldn't help being good at capturing.

"Fine," said Mr. O'Hara.

"You draw a card?" Henry asked Mr. O'Hara.

"As a matter of fact, no," said Mr. O'Hara.

"Aw!" groaned a couple of kids.

But then he patted his jacket pocket, as if he had something in there. "Now would you take out your copies of *Light in the Forest*? Let's remember that the game goes on during recess and lunch, but *not during class.*" Mr. O'Hara already had his book open, and he fished an extra copy from his desk drawer and handed it to Christina.

I sat in my seat, my blood racing, staring at the back of Christina's head. Hadn't anybody else noticed how she froze people when she captured them?

"You can follow along with us," Mr. O'Hara said to Christina.

Norton sat with us at lunch again. "We're touching ankles, Norton, just in case you've got any ideas," said Rachel.

"I'm not after any of you guys." Norton opened his wrinkled brown paper bag and took out his usual salami and onion sandwich.

"Who have you got?" asked Rachel.

"Jennifer Akers." Norton took a bite of his sandwich.

"Look at her now," said Amy. Christina was standing with three or four boys and holding her bundle of cards and shaking her head.

"Have you watched what happens when she catches somebody?" I asked. "She hypnotizes them. Watch her." Naturally, she wasn't after anyone right then.

"Better not let her catch you," said Amy to Norton.

"Ha, ha, I don't intend to."

"Wait, look, there she goes," I said. Christina was chasing Dan Fields. He lunged toward the middle of the lunchroom, and Christina caught him there. He seemed to turn to wax for a moment, then he handed her his cards without a word.

"Did you see *that*?" I asked.

"She does kind of stun people, doesn't she," said Rachel. "But look—Dan's all right now." He looked perfectly normal. "Speaking of all right, how's your uncle, Norton?"

"He's woken up a few times, but so far he goes right back out again. I'm going to go see him tonight."

"I'll bet you he's going to be okay," said Rachel, and I added, "Why don't you call me after you get to see him, if it isn't too late?"

"Not to change the subject," said Rachel, "but I just saw Michael Morris, Amy, if you're interested."

"Where?"

"The table in front of the blackboard."

"Come with me?"

We left our lunches half-eaten and linked hands and stumbled and squeezed past the metal lunchroom chairs. Michael Morris was sitting alone at a table, with a sweatshirt on the chair beside him. He was chewing a peanut butter sandwich and swinging one foot and talking to himself as he turned through a stack of baseball cards. "This is saved," he said, putting his hand on the chair as we piled up behind him. "Oh no!" He caught on as Amy put her hand on his shoulder. "I was eating! Not fair!"

"Sorry, but it is fair," said Amy, a grin working its way across her face. "This is sort of fun."

Michael's eyes brimmed with tears.

"This always happens the first time you play," said Norton.

Amy looked at the card Michael handed her. He had bent it and straightened it so many times, it was all smudged. "Alice Pepper."

"She's a twin," said Michael in between sniffs. "I couldn't figure out how to tell which one she was."

"Sixth grade," said Amy. "I know them." She shook her hair back, and I had the impression she was trying to imitate Christina, probably without meaning to. That's the thing about Amy—one minute she's following me; the next, she gets side-tracked and follows someone else.

"What'll I do about Mr. Bonner?" Rachel pouted. "He never comes out of his office at lunchtime."

The lunchroom was a madhouse by now, with

kids shrieking and squealing as they ran around in chaotic lines and bunches, stumbling and jerking each other along. Food was getting knocked to the floor. "A bit much this year, isn't it?" I heard Mr. Spencer say to Miss Grabill. They had been on lunch duty all week, but today they had stationed themselves at the very edge of the room, by the exit to the playground.

"Let's clear off our table and go outside," I said. Norton had sat down next to Michael. "Do you want the rest of your lunch?" I asked Norton.

"Sure," he said. "Thanks."

I hadn't meant that I would bring it to him!

But I did anyhow. Rachel and Amy and I hooked hands and pushed our way back to our original table, and I gathered up the remains of Norton's sandwich and cookies, and we took them back to where he was sitting. "Thanks, woman," he said. I gave him a little kick in the ankle, which I knew he was expecting, and then the three of us ran through the lunchroom doors and outside. It was wild. Shouts and screams rang all around us, and you could see kids looking desperate as they tried to hold on to each other. They would all lunge together at some lone child who had lost his grip. The littlest kids, watching from the safety of their sand play lot, looked scared to death.

On the far side of the playing fields there is a grassy slope that marks the edge of Oak Hill's borders. We ran all the way across to the hill and up to the top and fell down on the grass. From there you could see what everybody else was doing on the entire playground. Swarms of kids kept bunching up and spreading out and dividing around the swings and the seesaw and the painted hopscotch squares. On the soccer field little toy children raced up and down, swarming like ants, kicking a tiny sugar ball. We could make out Christina darting among them, her hair like a silver arrow.

"They're hysterical," said Rachel.

"Does anybody know who has any of us?" I asked.

"Nope," said Amy. "Hey, look. Haven't you got her card? Hey, Molly!" She got to her feet and waved. Molly Frick looked up at us through round, glittering glasses. She was carrying a sketchbook under one arm—probably working on the yearbook.

"She'll be easy," Amy said to me. "Hey, you said we had to play, didn't you?"

It made me a little sick to think of capturing Molly. Once I caught someone, that meant I was committed to the game. But I was the one who had said we had to play, wasn't I? I got up and waved along with Amy. "Come on, Molly! Put us in a sketch! Listen, don't worry, we're not really playing this year. We've already decided to let ourselves get caught." Everyone agreed that if you wanted to win, you could use any trick you could think of—that was really part of the so-called fun—lying, pretending you didn't know who had your friend's card, anything except actually physically grabbing cards away or dragging people from their safety holds.

"Are you serious?" Molly came closer. She was so shy, she hardly ever talked to anyone. I could guess that sometimes she wished we were her friends the way we sometimes wanted to be the Duckies' friends. She was going to be easy to fool.

"It's a little kids' game," I said. "We're going to let Norton win. Or that new girl."

Molly tucked her sketch pad under her arm and climbed through the tall grass, her feet splaying out awkwardly against the steep slope. When she got to the top, she sat down on the ground, and we sat down with her. "It's nice up here," she said. My stomach gave a little twist, but I went ahead. I could be extra nice to Molly some other time.

"Let's all cross our ankles, just in case. Somebody could sneak up from behind," I said. So we did. Molly flipped over her half-done drawing and started a fresh page.

"That's so good," said Amy. "Do you take art lessons?"

Molly was good. In five minutes the outlines of the school buildings were shaped across the page; in the distance she penciled in a couple of boys chasing each other across the grass. Then the bell began to ring.

"You can come back to the door with us," I offered. Molly held out her hand. The four of us half-ran, half-stumbled down the hill and across the field. Chains of kids were converging on the back door, squealing and stepping on each other. Once I saw a mother pig in a zoo with a litter of twelve piglets, and they sounded just like that.

At the back door, Molly looked hesitantly off to the right, where her classroom was. "Want me to come with you?" I said. "We'll find somebody else." I let go of Amy, and Amy grabbed for a teacher. I set off with Molly, and a moment later I dug my fingers into some boy's jacket sleeve—I didn't even know who he was. The three of us jostled along toward the seventh grade, and then the boy inside the jacket jerked away, and Molly said, "Oh!" in a tiny baby voice. I decided this was as good a time as any. "I've got you!" I said, and pulled out the crumpled card.

Molly turned red. "You said you weren't really playing!"

"I am, though. Sorry. You have to give me your card." I had grabbed Molly's wrist and was holding on to it. The Duckies swept by, all smoothly linked, all looking right at me. Then they looked at each other, and sly little grins came across their faces, and Claire said, "Keep it up, Zoe." "Good for you!" said Elizabeth.

I heard the sarcasm behind their sugary words.

I took Molly's card. It had Norton's name on it, of all people.

CHAPTER SIX

School was pretty chaotic the rest of that day. Other years, Norton had loved playing the game, and he'd run around like a madman, catching people. But this time, so far, he wasn't going after anyone. I was sure he had his mind on his uncle. I hadn't heard anything yet about who had my card. Usually by this point, kids are beginning to know who has whose card; people tell, and little subwars and substrategies start up. I couldn't help noticing Christina and how good she was at fitting in at our school, or appearing to fit in, anyway. This probably sounds pretty sour, but I couldn't believe people really liked her that much. It was just that she acted as if they did, so everyone thought everyone *else* liked her. Up close she seemed far away, you might say. Her eyes were bright, but you couldn't read her feelings in them. If she had any.

Rachel and Amy and I hooked onto each other to go from history to French. All the yelling and laughing and plunging around started up again the moment the bell sounded. The game was always chaos, but this time it felt different. Everyone was taking it too seriously. And it was moving so fast. Kids were in a frenzy.

When we got to French, the three of us had to unhook ourselves, because we weren't all in the same class, but I thought at the time that everything was okay. We had all promised each other we'd be careful, and if we weren't linked together, we were going to be sure to join some other line of kids. At the end of French we met again and headed for our lockers. The game was over for the day, and you could tell that everybody was relieved. As I was getting my things together, I remembered about the photograph.

"Don't wait for me," I said to Amy and Rachel. "I'm going up to the front office. Want to go to the mall tomorrow?" This was our Saturday ritual.

"Sure," said Rachel. "Call me later."

"I'll see," said Amy. "I don't feel good. Listen, I got caught. I'm sorry! I couldn't help it."

"Who was it?" I asked.

"Christina." She shrugged her shoulders and looked embarrassed.

"I thought we were all going to be careful!" I said.

"It was right when French began. So now she'll be after that twin, Alice Pepper. I have a terrible headache. I feel sort of dizzy. Maybe it's the pollen."

She did look sick—her face was white and strained-looking.

"Well, when she caught you, did you...feel anything strange?" I asked.

She shook her head. "I can't remember."

"My mom'll give you a ride," said Rachel. They left together.

I waited fifteen minutes or so, until the halls were emptied of kids. Christina didn't show up at her locker. I started for the front office, with the faded photo in my hand. Mrs. Webster sits in a little office in front of Mr. Bonner's big office, running interference for him. You can't get to Mr. Bonner unless Mrs. Webster says so.

I walked straight along the corridor as fast as I could go. What was I going to say? I didn't really know. Ahead of me at the end of the corridor was a flight of stairs that led up to the main entrance of the school. I thought I heard someone walking behind me. I looked back, but there was only a little boy down by the second grade, going to his cubby. I straightened around and kept walking, bumping my knuckles every now and then against the metal lockers. Yes, there was the sound again. Someone was behind me; the footsteps nearly matched mine, but they fell a split second after. I looked back. No one. I began to walk faster, my knees and back stiff, hurrying like a stork. I hoped no one had seen me going along like this, looking so ridiculous. How long was the stupid corridor, anyway?

Finally I grabbed the banister at the foot of the stairs and ran up, pulling myself with one hand, taking the stairs two at a time. At the top I turned around and called, "Who's there?"

A library aide, a parent volunteer, went past me, pushing a huge cart of books. The woman glanced down the empty stairs and gave me a questioning look. I could see a delivery man arriving, pushing backward through the front door, his arms stacked with cartons.

I walked toward the glass partition where Mrs. Webster presided.

Mrs. Webster looked up from her desk, an array of pale plastic machines, her computer humming in the background. "What do you want, dear? Shouldn't you be heading home?" A door behind her was open, and Mr. Henkes, the custodian, and two men with wrenches were doing something to the pipes. Everywhere around Mrs. Webster were stacks of papers, and most of them looked wet. "We had a flood in the records closet Tuesday night, and we're still trying to clean up."

"I wanted to ask you something about that new girl," I said. "It sounds strange, but I don't think she really went here before. I had this class picture, but now it's all faded and you can't see who's in it. Do you actually remember her?"

"Well, I don't know, I was leaving all that to Miss Albrecht. I don't remember her from before, myself, and I can usually keep pretty good track of who's been here. But we're kind of distracted. First there was the flood, and now there's some virus going around. I suppose it's hit your class. All kinds of kids were coming down with it today. Some of them went home early—that cute little Josh Perkins, and Mrs. Thompson, I'm afraid."

Out of the corner of my eye, I saw a sweep of silver hair at the top of the stairs. At the same moment, Mr. Bonner's door opened and he stepped across the threshold with a piece of paper in his hand.

"Look out!" I screamed. I don't know why, because the game was officially not supposed to be played after school hours. People do start to push the rules, though, almost as soon as the game gets going. Mr. Bonner and Mrs. Webster both jumped a mile, and I dashed around Mrs. Webster's desk and grabbed her wrist with one hand and Mr. Bonner's coat sleeve with the other. For a moment we were safe; then Mr. Bonner shrank back, shaking me off, and Christina laid her hand on Mrs. Webster's shoulder.

"I've got you," she said.

"Not that blasted game," grumped Mr. Bonner. He retreated into his office, closing the door behind him.

Christina was showing Mrs. Webster the card she had in her hand.

"It doesn't count if it's not during school," I said, sounding squeaky. "Those are the rules. We have to play by the rules!"

Mrs. Webster's attention was fixed on Christina. "Oh, let's let it go this one time. She's new," she said. She gave Christina the card she'd tucked beneath her blotter. "Besides, the sooner we're done with this, the better. Mr. Bonner hates all the fuss and wasted class time."

"But it shouldn't—," I started to say. Christina moved out of the office at triple speed, and I chased after her. I don't know what I had in mind, but it made me mad that she could talk a grown-up into breaking the rules so easily. "Wait!" I called.

She didn't slow down. She seemed to float down

the main stairs and then along the hall that led to our lockers. I raced along behind her. Christina opened her locker door and stepped in back of it; it looked as if she was putting something in or taking something out of the bottom of her locker. I ran the last few steps and grabbed the edge of the open door and looked behind it. In the shadow of the door a huge swarm of sparks, like a spiral of gnats, had eaten away one of Christina's shoulders. It looked as if the whole left side of her body was about to dissolve; and then part of her face looked over at me and immediately her body began to fill back out. My face burned. I blinked my eyes, seeing purple dots, the way you do when a flashbulb goes off in your face, and it took a moment to get my eyesight back. Then Christina was complete again, bending down, pushing something into her locker. She shut the door and stood up and looked at me and said, "Don't tell."

CHAPTER SEVEN

I had to walk home by myself, and I counted every single step it took. I was afraid to run, but I was afraid to go slowly, too. I kept wanting to look back, but I was afraid if I did, that would make something appear that I didn't want to see.

My mother was out when I got home. I locked the front door and sat down on the couch for a few minutes, trying to convince myself that I hadn't seen what I had seen. Maybe something had gone wrong with my eyes—but then why would Christina have said "Don't tell"? I went around the house to make sure all the windows were shut. Then I dialed Norton's number; he wasn't there. Nobody was home at Rachel's either, and just as I started calling Amy, I remembered she'd been caught. Amy's mother answered the telephone. She said Amy was lying down, because she didn't feel well.

I wasn't feeling too good myself. I could tell the longer I waited, the more afraid I was going to get. I had to tell my parents. Maybe they would call the police, or some scientists—just call in some scientists and they would know what to do. I kept picturing it over and over in my mind—the pinpoints of light and then the way her body seemed to come through them and put itself together. If she could do it to herself, could she do it to other people? I held out my hand and wondered what it would be like to go back and forth from sparks, to your regular body, to sparks.

The silence in the house was awful.

I ran upstairs to my room and pulled down the shade so I couldn't see out and nothing could see in. I sat on my bed and listened for the tiniest noise. What I heard, embarrassing to say, was my stomach growling. I was hungry. I'd have given anything for a big slice of chocolate cake with chocolate frosting and a glass of milk. I started down the hall to go to the kitchen for a snack, but as I reached the top step, I heard something. Something definite. It was a creak and a crash downstairs, like a footstep and then someone dropping something, or else it was the defroster in the refrigerator letting the ice crash to the drip tray, or it could have been the floor-boards creaking, the way they always do in old houses like ours.

I wasn't about to go down to find out. I ran back to my room and slammed the door. A few minutes later the front door opened and closed. This time there was no mistaking the sound. Why hadn't I remembered to lock the door? But I *had* locked the door.

It was my mother.

A cheerful call floated up to my ears: "Zoe? I'm home. Are you upstairs?"

"Hi!" It came out sounding half-strangled. I went to the top of the stairs and ran down. I was so happy to hear the ordinary noises of grocery bags rustling, my mom's shoes clicking on the floor, the soft thump as she let her purse fall onto a chair. I wouldn't even have cared if she was in the worst mood ever.

"You're never going to believe what happened to me today," I said.

Christina's warning whispered itself through my ears: "Don't tell."

"What was that?" There was no telling how she would react to what I was going to say.

"Well, you know that new girl I was telling you about? She's been acting like she's so friendly, and trying to get to be friends with everyone? Today I followed her down the hall and saw her by accident in front of her locker, and she wasn't a human being. She was partly turning into sparks. Like, you know, an alien." I flinched when I said the word *alien*; it sounded so melodramatic.

"What happened again?"

"I saw her behind the locker door, and she had partly turned into sparks, dots of light, swirling around." I might not even believe it myself if I was hearing it for the first time.

"You must have been having some visual problem, don't you think?"

"She told me not to tell, Mom. She knew she was doing it." By now I was sounding weak as a kitten.

"Aliens?" My mother began to fold up the grocery bags very fast, flattening them so crisply along their corners that I knew she was annoyed. When she gets worried, she gets annoyed. If she gets very worried, she gets very annoyed. "Is this some kind of joke? I don't understand, Zoe."

"Neither did I, but it really happened. She got into Oak Hill somehow, you know, not the regular way. And Mrs. Webster can't remember her."

"Well, Zoe, that doesn't mean the girl is an alien!"

"But what about the sparks?"

"Migraines run in our family. I could make a doctor's appointment for you, if you like."

"No."

"Now, what did you hear about Norton's uncle? Any more news?"

I told her what I could. I tried to steer the conversation back to Christina. "Want me to tell you what she said?" I offered.

"Why don't we discuss it when your father gets home," she said.

So when we were all eating dinner, I described what had happened again. "I saw that new girl dissolve behind her locker. I think she's...well, an alien." *Clink.* My father put the bottle of salad dressing on its saucer. When he's really concerned about something, he gets very quiet and slow.

"What did you say?" he asked.

"I saw the new girl change into sparks. Just her shoulder and her face. Nobody else was around, just her and me."

"You must have been having a hallucination," my mother put in.

"How do you know if you are?" I asked.

"So no one else saw her?" asked my father.

"No. It was late, and I came right home; I didn't want to stay there any longer."

"Was there some overhead light that burned out right then?"

"Nope."

My parents ate a few slow bites without saying anything. I could see past them out the kitchen window, where the air was that deep blue color that lingers and lingers until suddenly the night is black. I saw a spark of light between houses, quite far away; it could have been the taillight on a car. You'd never know if someone was out there watching and listening while we trapped spaghetti on our forks and swallowed ice water and poked through the salad for another cube of cucumber.

"Why don't we go shopping for a new stove tonight?" said my mother. She was probably thinking this would get rid of the whole subject.

"I'm coming along," I said.

"I wonder if we should all stay in this evening and look for a stove some other time," said my father.

"No," said my mother, "you and I both need to go, and the stores will be crowded tomorrow."

"There's no way I'm staying here by myself," I said.

"We'll all go, then," said my father. "If you start to feel sick or see this thing again, you tell us right away."

I followed them all evening like a four-year-old, up and down the aisles of appliances at Wonder Mart. They didn't decide on a stove.

CHAPTER EIGHT

What I usually do on weekends is go over to Rachel's. Most times Amy comes, too, and we dye our hair, or paint our fingernails ten different colors, or bake cookies and eat half the dough. The Flahertys have a large and usually chaotic household, and a few episodes of pink hair don't even attract notice.

This Saturday I got dressed and went downstairs before my parents were up. I drank a glass of juice, made some toast, and called up to them, "I'll be at Rachel's." I was out the door before my father had come down to start the coffee. I walked the whole ten blocks to the Flahertys', thinking how clear and clean everything seemed in the morning light. Saturday's my favorite day of the week, and I was really hoping I could enjoy it without having to get all scared and anxious again. I decided I must have been seeing things after all.

Mrs. Flaherty answered the door. She had on jeans and a turtleneck and deerskin moccasins. "Come on in and have some breakfast with us. Rachel said you might be over."

I followed Mrs. Flaherty to the kitchen. Mixed smells of bacon and coffee and burned toast warmed the room. Mr. Flaherty, his striped bathrobe tied around his ample stomach, was stirring eggs in a huge black frying pan. Rachel was perched on a high stool, cradling a piece of toast. Her six-year-old brother, Marshall, was eating cereal at one end of the table, and Tim, in an undershirt and blue jeans, was standing over the toaster, ready to flick up the lever.

"Zoe! Have some scrambled eggs!" boomed Mr. Flaherty.

"That's okay. I've eaten."

"Have an English muffin, then," said Mr. Flaherty. "Tim, give that one to Zoe."

The toaster gave a prolonged *twang* as Tim popped up the muffin halves.

"Why does it do that?" asked Marshall.

"It's going to blow up," said Tim. He mashed margarine onto the halves and put them on the bare tabletop in front of me. Mrs. Flaherty handed across a clean plate. Tim put in another English muffin.

"What do you two have planned for today?" asked Mrs. Flaherty. "Jordan has a game this afternoon, if you want to go to that."

"I'm going!" Marshall said.

"We're all going," said Mrs. Flaherty.

Tim looked over his shoulder and shook his head, mouthing the word *no*.

"We haven't decided what we're doing yet, have we, Zoe?" Rachel gave me a look. It was important to stay uncommitted when you were at the Flahertys', or the next thing you knew you'd be in the backseat of their van, rattling along the highway toward a pick-your-own apple orchard or a community cleanup day in someone else's community.

"So how's the new girl?" Tim said to me. "Rachel says she's a knockout."

"Yeah," I said. "She's such a knockout, it makes you wonder if she's real." My stomach gave a twist, and a lump of dread moved in, and there went Saturday.

"She's not that great," said Rachel. "But it's true everything about her is so *perfectly smooth*."

"I know," I said. "She's so perfect, she might not be real. She might be an alien!" I couldn't help saying it, just to get the words out, even though I made it sound like I was joking.

"An *alien?*" said Marshall. A Cheerio fell out of his mouth.

Mr. and Mrs. Flaherty laughed.

"She's really weird," I said.

"I'll tell you something weird," said Tim. "I read about this school where one day all the kids disappeared."

"What?" Mrs. Flaherty sounded surprised.

"Cross my heart. The whole school vanished, poof, gone."

"Tim, you are full of it," said Rachel, but she wasn't smiling.

"Just the people, not the buildings. Not the chalk. Not the erasers."

"Little kids, too?" asked Marshall.

"Especially the little kids!"

"Timothy, stop scaring your brother. What a lot of nonsense. Marshall, people do not disappear, and nothing's going to happen to you at Oak Hill." Mrs. Flaherty gave Tim a disgusted look. "Now, where did you hear this story, or did you make it up?"

"I read it in one of those junk papers—*The Chronicle.* It was a while ago, Mom. A few months ago. I knew *I* didn't have to worry, because no high school kids went there. Only the *little* kids got taken." He leaned over and winked at Marshall, who let out a mock wail.

"Can't you find something decent to read?" asked Mr. Flaherty.

"I thought you guys didn't believe anything in those papers anyhow," said Tim. "You said it's all made up."

"Where did they go when they got taken?" whispered Marshall.

"There. You see?" said Mrs. Flaherty. "Now we'll be hearing about this for weeks." She sighed.

"Marshall, it can't be true," said Tim, giving him a hearty pat on the shoulders. "Besides, it was in Peru or someplace really far away. Hey, can I be excused?"

"Not a moment too soon," said his mother.

Tim pushed himself back from the table, put his plate in the sink, and went out the back door. I could hear a basketball bouncing on the driveway.

"Thanks for the muffin," I said. "May I be excused?" I saw a faint smile creep across Rachel's face, and she gave me a look. I put my plate in the sink, too, and went out to the Flahertys' back steps and sat down to watch Tim shoot baskets.

Tim hurled the ball at me. I caught it, hopped down the stairs, and bounced it a few times on the driveway. I took a shot. The ball ricocheted off the backboard. Tim darted forward, grabbed it, spun around, and shot. The ball missed, bounced off the backboard again.

"I've got it!" I shouted. Tim got there first and stuck out his rear end to bump me away. He swung the ball around, and I grabbed the back of his shirt and locked one arm around his elbow.

"What?" he said. He shook me off and took a shot. This time the ball dropped straight into the basket with a splash of net.

"You can't do that twice," I said.

"You can't do it once," Tim said.

"Let me try." I was starting to feel better bouncing the ball around. I was dribbling it pretty well when Tim snaked his hand in and slapped it away. He raced toward the basket and threw a hook shot that missed and went sailing over the neighbors' stockade fence and landed on something with a *thwack.* "Hey!" came a voice from behind the fence. "What do you think we have a fence for?"

Mr. Whitman's bald head, topped by two sprigs of hair, appeared above the row of pointed posts. He surveyed the driveway, holding the ball up for us to see. "I've half a mind to hang on to this," he said.

"Sorry," said Tim. "I don't know how it got over there."

"I do," said Mr. Whitman. He tossed the ball to Tim. Tim shot again, to show that he wasn't intimidated; then he sat down on the top step and put the ball beside him. I settled on the next step down and measured a crack with the side of my shoe.

"Did you believe that article?" I asked.

Rachel came out of the back door and sat down beside me.

Tim shrugged. "When I read it, I thought it *could* happen."

"That's what I was thinking," I said. "Lots of things *could* happen. Like about the alien. What if that new girl really was one? She *could* be. What if she, you know, dissolved?"

Tim stood up and dribbled the ball several times, as if the *rat-a-tat* noise would drive out all this nonsense.

"How could she dissolve?" asked Rachel. "She looked pretty solid to me."

"Turn into dots of light, something weird like that." I suddenly saw again Christina's single eye looking at me from part of her face in the shadow of the locker door.

"Want to hear something else weird?" asked Tim. "You know that old school up on Chickatawbut? Bet you don't know what they say about it."

"What do they say?" I asked.

"That it closed down because of some kind of epidemic. There are these rumors."

"What rumors?" I asked.

"Something wiped it out, though the school tried

to cover up for it. They say if you can get over the fence and look around, there's something up there, some secret."

"Oh, come on, Tim," said Rachel. "Everybody's heard that. It's just something kids say. The police would know, or somebody would, if there was something dangerous up there."

"Maybe they would, maybe they wouldn't. Kids can keep secrets among themselves."

"But what is it?" I practically shouted.

"I haven't been up there. Some people think it's a nest of some sort."

"A *nest?*" I said. "There're probably all sorts of nests up there, it's been abandoned so long."

"So what was it, a nest of killer bees?" said Rachel.

Tim started to bounce the basketball again, then tried to palm it. It slipped from his outstretched fingers. "They say if you touch it, you die!" He had dropped his voice to a horror-movie whisper.

"Want to go to the mall?" Rachel asked me.

"Sure," I said. "Least there won't be any killer bees."

"Want a ride?" asked Tim.

"Who with?" I said.

"Me."

"You can't drive yet!"

"Correction. I can drive. I just don't have my license."

"Good-bye, Tim," said Rachel firmly.

We took the bus to the mall after the Flahertys left for Jordan's game.

"Did you talk to Amy since yesterday?" I asked as we swayed and bumped along.

"I tried calling her, but her mom said she was still sick and she'd gone to bed."

"Maybe we ought to go see her later."

"Yeah."

We both stared out the window, silent the rest of the way.

We always went to our favorite stores at the mall in a certain order. First we tried on purple blazers in Yours Truly while a salesclerk in cowboy boots and size-five jeans watched our every move. Then we breezed through Bernard's, the expensive department store, stopping to let ourselves be sprayed with perfume. A pro basketball team was doing a fund-raiser shoot-around by the escalators, so we hung over the balcony rail and watched several seven-foot men in gold satin shorts shoot baskets. Then we ordered french fries and diet sodas in the snack atrium. So far we hadn't seen anyone we knew.

Rachel spent a long time browsing in the

makeup aisle at the discount drugstore. She finally picked out some transparent mascara and a turquoise eyeliner pencil. I picked up two bottles of apricot face scrub, which I use all the time, because it's for "problem skin," as they put it, and then I wandered over to the racks of magazines and newspapers. There in the tabloids section was *The Chronicle* with a big black headline: SPACE VISITOR LEAVES MOM SPEECHLESS. I picked it up and started reading: *At her kitchen table sat a thing with a smooth head and lizardlike body, round pads for feet, colored green all over, with a pulsing throat. It put its pads on her face and asked for food and water, speaking perfect English.*

"I doubt it," I said out loud.

"What?" Rachel looked over my shoulder.

"Any alien that's smart enough to get here wouldn't come looking like that," I said.

"Speaking of aliens," muttered Rachel. Three of the Duckies were working their way up the aisle from the other end. They stopped at a display of foot remedies and burst into giggles at something in a yellow package.

"Hi! Oh, hi!" they said when they saw us.

"Whatcha reading?" asked Claire, coming up to me. I noticed her tiny silver earrings, shaped like leaping frogs. All the Duckies wore them.

"I love this paper," I said. "It's got everything—

aliens, rock stars, horoscopes." Claire gave an appreciative chuckle, the Duckie sign of approval, and in spite of myself I felt a little blip of happiness: I had passed inspection.

"Hey," said Elizabeth. "Look over there. Isn't that—?"

Christina was standing by the shelves of soap.

I went cold all over, and Rachel said, "Uh-oh" under her breath. Christina was holding two bottles of apricot face scrub.

"I was hoping I'd meet somebody I knew," Christina said. "What's going on?" Her eyes met mine, and she smirked ever so faintly.

"Just hanging out," said Tam.

"This is a great mall," Christina said, nodding her head.

"We come here a lot," Elizabeth said.

"Everybody does," said Rachel.

"You want to ask her to...?" Tam said to her friends. The Duckies exchanged glances among themselves and cracked their gum feelingly. Sometimes they didn't bother finishing their sentences.

"I'm getting this." Christina held up the face scrub.

"You've got the same stuff she does," Elizabeth said to me, as if I was the one copying Christina.

I shrugged. "Plus this," I said, holding out *The*

Chronicle. "It's got an article about an alien."

Christina looked a little tense. "Oh, aliens," she said. "I saw an alien once."

"You did?" Elizabeth looked as though she was having second thoughts about Christina.

"He looked like Mr. O'Hara," said Christina, giving me another sly glance.

"Oh no!" said Tam, and they all laughed.

"Mr. O'Hara is definitely *not* an alien!" said Claire. "Mr. Bonner, now, he's a different story!"

The three of them shrieked with laughter.

"Want to come to the movies with us this afternoon?" Elizabeth asked Christina. "If you're not already..." Elizabeth gave me a sideways look, as if to say, I know this is rude, but so what, I can get away with it.

"Sure," said Christina. They began to arrange a meeting time. The way things work at our school, they expected Rachel and me to melt away, and that's pretty much what we did. We all got in line to pay for our makeup and soap. Christina was ahead of me, but she stepped back and waved me past her. I didn't know why. I went ahead, thinking I could hardly wait to leave anyhow. She stood so close to me when I was paying, I could feel her breath; she was watching everything I did. When she opened her bag, I saw that she didn't have a wallet, but she did have her bundle of Elimination cards with her. I couldn't help laughing. "Ready to play right now?" I said, not caring if I sounded nasty. Why would anyone carry their cards with them on the weekend? Unless they were truly a nerd, or a fanatic. The Duckies looked a little surprised, too.

"I forgot I had these with me," said Christina. "Everything is so confused; we're still moving in."

"Where's your wallet?" I asked.

She blinked as if she didn't know what I was talking about.

"Want to borrow some money?" Elizabeth offered.

"Sure," Christina said.

"Let them have her," Rachel said to me as we headed for the bus stop. She sounded fed up.

"Fine with me," I said.

We got off the bus at a stop a couple of blocks from Amy's house and went up to her front door. Mrs. Johnson let us in. "She's got some kind of virus, I think," she said. "She doesn't have a fever, though; in fact, she's subnormal. Go on up for a few minutes, but don't get too close—you don't want to catch it."

Amy looked sick as a dog. She was tucked way down in her bed with the covers pulled up to her nose. We stood in the doorway and waved to her, and she opened her eyes halfway. "Don't get this," she said. "I'm so tired, and I can't eat. It's so weird, because I love to eat. I'm too tired to eat."

"We've been to the mall," said Rachel.

"That new girl was there," I said.

"I've got to be okay by Monday," said Amy. "I've got to go back to school on Monday."

"You'll be well by then," said Rachel. She can sound as soothing as anyone's mother.

"Want us to bring you anything?" I asked.

"I'm going to sleep now," said Amy, and her eyes closed right then as we were looking at her.

Rachel shrugged at me, and we tiptoed back downstairs. "Would you tell her to call us if she starts to feel better?" Rachel said to Mrs. Johnson.

"Or if she wants some company?" I added, and we left.

We went back to the bus stop, and while we were waiting I had to tell Rachel I was serious about thinking Christina could be an alien. "You know what we were talking about this morning with Tim? Out on the steps? You're going to think I'm crazy, but it was real, Rachel. On Friday I saw Christina turn into sparks of light. I'm sure she's an alien, though it sounds so...!" I threw up my hands, since I couldn't think of a good word for it. "She gets into my house and sees what I'm doing."

"Are you positive?" Rachel said after a moment. "How do you know?"

I told her about the catalog and the yogurt and the creepy sense I had that she was copying me.

"But why would an alien stand in line in the drugstore and buy apricot face scrub?" Rachel asked.

"Maybe she didn't know what else to do. Maybe she had to follow what I was doing."

"I've got that catalog at home, too. I'm going to look at it again."

"You'll see what I mean."

"But how do you know you weren't seeing things with the sparks?"

The bus came and stopped with a weighty hiss. We climbed on, and Rachel kept talking. "Maybe when she said, 'Don't tell,' she meant don't tell that she was hanging around after school. Maybe she was, you know, putting away a pack of cigarettes and thought you saw her and that's why she said that."

"I don't know," I said. "I mean, I don't know what aliens can do. They can do anything, can't they?"

"It just seems so unlikely, you know?" Rachel glanced out the bus window. "We're almost there. Want to come over for a while?"

"Not really." I was starting to feel upset.

"You must have been mistaken, Zoe. It's such a remote possibility."

"Well, I know it's a remote *possibility*," I said. The thought that she didn't believe me wormed a hollow through my stomach.

On the other hand, what if she was right? How likely was it that an alien could be walking around in North Point?

"Zoe, don't be mad. Let's not have a fight. Come on. Tim's probably there." Her eyes crinkled in a teasing smile.

I shook my head. "I'm just going to go home."

Rachel waved at me from the sidewalk, and the bus doors flapped shut. I studied the people bumping along on the bench across from me: an old lady wearing a sweater and a raincoat, holding the handle of a shopping bag full of what looked like old clothes; a mother trying to hold on to her squirming toddler—he would run up to a stranger and say "Hi!" and wait for a forced smile, then dart back to his mother; two white-haired men in windbreakers, discussing lettuce. The bus roared and a whorl of exhaust fumes poured out behind us; cars honked and swerved around us. We pulled over to the curb, and I swung down the steps and out onto the sidewalk. This was my street, with front yards I knew by heart, and the red octagonal stop sign on the corner, and the manhole cover with the tree shape stamped in it. It didn't seem like a spot for aliens.

CHAPTER NINE

When I came in the door, I could see that my mother had been cleaning. The kitchen counters were clear of the usual clutter, and they gleamed under the light. Something was baking in the oven, and a can of chocolate frosting sat by the fruit bowl. Mom was sitting at the table reading a magazine.

"Where'd you go? The mall?" she asked.

"Yep."

"How was it?"

"Fine."

"What'd you do?"

"Just looked around. Some other kids were here—that new girl."

My mother put down the magazine slowly. "You mean the one you told me about?"

"That one. I don't know. Rachel and I were talking about it. She doesn't think I could have seen that what I told you about."

My mom looked relieved. "That's my opinion too. We could take you for an eye checkup, you know, especially if it happens again."

"Right." It seemed easier to go along with her but as soon as I did, an odd little fear began to beat like a toy drum in a corner of my mind. I sometimes get a headache this way—it starts faintly and goes off and on, but it never goes away entirely, and then it gets stronger and stronger, just when I think I can forget about it.

"Your father and I are going out to a movie tonight. We won't be late, though." Her voice seemed far away.

"Can I come with you?" I asked.

"Come out with us? Again?"

"What movie is it?"

Battleship Potemkin.

"I've always wanted to see that."

"Zoe! You've never heard of it! It was made even before I was born."

"Old movies are always the best."

"Well, your dad and I are going to have a night out by ourselves. You had a phone call, by the way. A boy. I said you'd call him back."

"You said *I* would call *him*? Mom!"

"Norton Peabody."

"Oh."

"I'm baking a cake, your favorite kind," my mother went on.

I didn't say anything.

"Zoe, I won't feel right about going out unless I know you feel okay," she said.

"I'm fine." I sighed. The drumbeat was soft but insistent.

The timer went off, and Mom took a chocolate cake out of the oven. She poked it with a toothpick, then left it on the counter to cool.

My parents left at 6:30. I heated up some leftover fried rice and cut a large piece of the cake. The house was quiet. I stood in the kitchen and looked out the window into the settling blue dusk. Black trees were overhanging the sidewalk, their thin new leaves fluttering in lonesome drafts, and I thought how everybody who was going home was already home. There weren't any people with bulging shopping bags walking from the bus; no little kids begged for one more run up the sidewalk on their Rollerblades.

Then I saw something luridly neon green, pulsing and blinking in the fence by the driveway. My heart gave a huge, billowing knock. Had I summoned it up just by thinking about it? I turned away, and I could hardly breathe, and then I caught sight of the digital clock we have under the kitchen cabinet. It was blinking green, the signal that it had to be reset. What I saw was only its reflection in the window. I went over and pushed the buttons to reset it. My mom had probably unplugged it to use the mixer and forgot about it.

I picked up the phone and dialed Norton's number. His mother said he'd just come home from visiting his uncle in the hospital and that she was about to take her turn and go.

"How is he?" I asked. "Is he going to be okay?"

"He's partly conscious, but still not back to normal," said Mrs. Peabody. "They're trying to figure out what actually happened. He doesn't have the sorts of injuries that come from being hit by lightning. It's something of a mystery."

"It is?" *Drum, drum, drum* went the beats, ever so softly.

"Here's Norton."

"Zoe—listen to what I did Friday."

"Wait'll you hear what I saw."

"Well, listen to this."

"Okay."

"Well. You know, Friday I started home on my

bike, and I was a little ways down the road when that car that picks up that new girl passed me, so I followed it. The one with the black windows? It's not exactly a limo, but what is it? I don't know what came over me, but I had some extra time. I rode along behind it because it was heading out Route Twenty, near where I live. I got as far as my street, and I started to turn off, but then I thought, What the heck, I might as well go a little farther. So I kept following it for a couple of miles, and it crossed Route Three and the expressway, and then it turned up toward Chester Hills reservation. I couldn't see it anymore, where the road starts to climb and curves a lot, but I thought I saw it stop and turn up Chickatawbut Hill Road. It only took me a minute to get that far, and by then all I could see was a taillight, way up high where the road reaches the top. But get this. The chain across the bottom was still there. I mean, it was still hooked to the post."

"Maybe she undid it," I said. My voice sounded thin.

"How could she? If she did, they couldn't have stopped, gotten out, unfastened it, driven through, gotten out again, fastened it again, all in a few seconds."

"Maybe the car drove around it."

"There's a lot of brush and trees planted there,

just to keep people from doing that."

"Ugh." I shivered with nervousness. "Why would she go up there? Even if she could get through, no one lives up there—there aren't any houses."

"There's that school; it used to be a boarding school. It closed eons ago, Uncle Arthur said, way back in the fifties."

A spiral of anxiety shot through me. "Listen to this." I told him about the sparks and my crazy fear about Christina, and I filled him in on the way she embodied things I thought about or did. Unlike everybody else I'd tried to tell, Norton loved it. He didn't take any convincing.

"You want to get your bike and ride up there?" he asked.

"Now?"

"Sure."

"But what if something's—"

"All we'll do is look around; we won't bother anything."

I went up to my room and found this really small flashlight that I got in my Christmas stocking. It fits on a key chain. I fastened the key chain through a belt loop on my jeans. Then I locked up the house and went out the back door. I took my bike out the side door of the garage, so I wouldn't be conspicuous. For a fleeting moment I wished I could just stay safely in the garage, with its familiar old-car smell. I straddled my bike and tested its headlight. Fortunately the battery wasn't dead. The beam of light it cast seemed awfully narrow, but then my eyes got used to the dark. It was a clear night, with plenty of stars, and soon it didn't even seem like I was riding in the dark.

When I got to Norton's house, he was waiting for me on his front porch. He was wearing scruffy old sweatpants and a ratty sweater, but his bike, a new mountain bike, gleamed all red and chrome under the streetlights.

It was a twenty-minute ride to the mountain. I had never gone all that way on my bike, though I've driven through Chester Hills plenty of times with my parents. I am out of shape, I found out immediately. I don't ride my bike much; it's an old ten-speed. I was gasping as we began to climb the paved main road that curves through the reservation. It didn't take long, though. We came to an inconspicuous dirt turnoff that led to a pair of steel posts linked by a thick metal chain. Norton stopped his bike and jumped off. CHICKATAWBUT HILL ROAD. PRIVATE. NO ADMITTANCE, read the rusty sign by the chain. I looked up the mountain. The dirt road rose into darkness. Nature groups sometimes come out here during the day—bird-watchers and wildflower watchers and so on. It was black now under the trees; there was a damp, mushroomy smell and the scent of new leaves. I heard a breeze blowing, but it sounded far off, as if the wind couldn't penetrate the woods.

Norton unhooked the chain at one end, and we pushed our bikes through. Then he stopped and re-hooked it to the post. We started pushing our bikes up the road.

"If nobody's supposed to get in here, how come there's a road?" I asked. Norton was leading the way, and I followed him as closely as I could without actually running into him. I did not want to let very much distance open up between us.

"It's probably left over from when the school was going," said Norton.

The hill was steep, and in a moment the entrance was out of sight. We kept our bike headlights on to show the way. The climbing was tough; it felt as if the road itself were resisting us. As we climbed higher, the road got narrower, until it was just a dirt lane. Everything was quiet, shielded by thick woods from the highway noises down below. A ditch fell away sharply on either side of the road, and trees and underbrush crowded up to its edges. We couldn't see anything past the wall of black leaves and jagged branches.

After a few minutes, Norton's headlight caught a small sign, half fallen from its stake and partly obscured by leaves. He pulled out his flashlight and clicked it on. The sign spelled out FERN RIDGE SCHOOL in chipped gold letters. A narrow track split off to the right. We followed it uphill. Now the tree branches were so overgrown, they touched overhead, and grass grew tall in the center of the road. It bent under our bike wheels, briefly showing green in our headlights as we passed over it. The air was colder up here than at the start of the trail. Noises came from the woods—a few birds, the rustle of an animal. I told myself it was a squirrel or a rabbit.

It got a little lighter up ahead as the trees thinned out, and then we came to a broad clearing where several cars could park. Before us rose a chain-link fence about ten feet tall, its gate fastened with a padlocked steel bar. Under the clear sky it gleamed like silver. We propped our bikes against it. "Guess we'll have to climb over," said Norton, and started up like a monkey. Through the fence I could glimpse an open meadow and some dark, low buildings at a distance. Once we were on the other side of the fence, it would be impossible to get out fast. But why would we need to? The drumbeats in my head gave a few soft raps. Well—there was no point in freaking myself out.

It was tricky getting footholds, because my feet basically were bigger than the diamond holes in the fence, but I managed to jam my toes partway through and pull myself up with my hands. At the top I had to be careful not to lose my balance swinging over, but getting down was a snap; and there we were, on top of the mountain. Beneath the stars a huge open space stretched before us, fragrant with tall grass and divided by an avenue of trees that ran toward the huddle of buildings. We walked slowly along the path, remnants of gravel crunching under our feet, such an everyday sound that I laughed. I sounded a little crazy.

"Over there is where it happened." Norton pointed toward the side of the clearing, away from the buildings, where there was an open place, a kind of elevated circle. "We had looked through a couple of windows in the school, just out of curiosity. Then he picked his spot and was setting up the telescope and I went back to the car."

It was warm up here, for some reason, though I remembered shivering on our way up. I smelled summer in the air—flowers and freshly mowed grass. I was starting to sweat.

Norton moved ahead of me toward the main building. It was a grand-looking place, with pillars and wings and carvings over the windows. Weeds grew through the cracks in the broken stone steps. Norton walked right up and tried the front door. It was locked, of course. I went over to a window and stood on tiptoe and looked in. There was a classroom with a couple of tilting wooden desks and a blank blackboard in the front.

"Let's go look around the back," said Norton.

We circled the main building, crossed some driveways and an overgrown yard, and reached a long building that looked like a dormitory. Through the windows I could see bunk beds shrouded with sheets to keep off dust. We moved along to a barn—locked with a huge padlock, and no windows—and some outbuildings that might have been garages and sheds for mowers. I put my face up close to a wide crack in the wall of the biggest one. I unhooked my flashlight and shone it into the crack; I could make out a tractor. Beside it was something that gleamed black; I couldn't see its shape.

"Look in here," I said. "What's parked on the other side of that tractor?"

Norton came up beside me and looked through the crack. "Looks like a car, a big black car. I can't see what make it is."

"Is there some other place to look through?" I walked quickly around the shed, scanning the walls for a bigger crack, but all the other boards were tightly fitted together.

I took another look, but I couldn't see much around the huge, muddy, grass-coated wheels of the tractor, just something with a sleek shape and a polished black surface.

I turned back. A bad feeling was gathering in my head and stomach. "I think we ought to go now," I said. "This place has definitely got something wrong with it."

"Want to go inside?" Norton nodded toward the main building. I could see a door open in the back— not just unlocked but standing open.

"I think we ought to go," I said. Panic was starting to take hold. "There's really something wrong up here."

"Let's just look for a moment," said Norton. "Nobody knows we're here. The police won't arrest us."

The sweet smell of mowed grass filled my nostrils. I didn't want to smell it anymore. It smelled like the wrong season; it reminded me of summer. It was too early in the spring to mow grass. I couldn't remember my dad getting out our mower yet from its winter storage spot in the basement. And who would be up here mowing? What for?

Norton was walking toward the central building. I didn't want to be left by myself, so I caught up with him. He stood at the threshold, whistling uncertainly and looking around. Inside, the building was totally black. Norton flicked on his flashlight, and the beam crawled along the hallway, lighting up door after door. "Come on," he said. I turned on my flashlight, too, so I could see where I was putting my feet.

It smelled funny inside—chalk and something musty and another sharply clean smell that reminded me of laundry. The fresh mountain air stopped at the entrance. Our feet crunched through dirt and dry leaves scattered across the wooden floor.

The first door we came to was shut. Norton opened it and stepped inside: just a classroom. There were desks in a circle, a partially erased blackboard, a book open, facedown, on the teacher's desk.

"Not much, is it," Norton said. The sound of his voice brought back everydayness for a moment— this was only an old stone school building, once grand, now abandoned.

I turned away and went toward another closed door. If Norton had the guts to open one, so did I. This classroom had math equations on the board. A few desks and chairs, thick dust that our feet brushed through. Every sound we made was magnified in the silence—my jeans rustled; my shoe creaked; I stumbled against a chair leg. It was *so* silent, as if something were holding its breath.

As soon as I thought that, I knew I was about to panic. I was really scaring myself. This is only an old school, I reminded myself. It's only a couple of minutes between here and the other side of the fence.

"You done?" I asked Norton. But he wasn't there when I looked behind me. "Norton?" I went to the door. Nobody in the hallway. *"Norton!"* I called.

"Come here," he said softly. A pale arm beckoned from a doorway far down the hall.

"What for?" My voice didn't seem to carry—maybe all the dust and leaves muffled the sound.

"Sssh."

By now the drums were really beating in my ears and my knees were getting shaky. I walked numbly down to the doorway where Norton beckoned. "Lookit," he said, and pointed to a gallon pickle jar sitting in the center of the teacher's desk. He shone his flashlight into it.

Fastened to the sides and covering the bottom were what looked like old cocoons, brown cylindrical things that you could see were hollow. Way up high, stuck to the bottom of the jar lid, were some small ones, with some tiny things flying around at a terrific speed right below them. They looked sort of like these hideous little brown moths that sometimes fly out of my mom's pantry, and then she has fits and cleans the entire thing and throws away all the flour and cake mix and cornmeal. "Mealy moths," I said. "Do you suppose this was a science classroom?"

I went closer to the jar. The critters flying around didn't seem to have wings; they were so small and quick, it was hard to see what they actually did look like. Then I thought I saw a blink of light come from one of them—it was so quick, I couldn't be sure.

"Fireflies?" I said.

"Don't touch it," Norton said, and he actually grabbed the back of my jacket. "Those things must have been hatching in there for years. Look at the top. There's dust all over it. Nobody's opened this jar since, I don't know, since the school closed."

"Let's go, Norton." Now the brown things were flying around faster. "Norton, I'm going." I didn't care about the jarful of bugs—even thinking about them made my scalp crawl. And I hated the quiet.

I began to walk down the hall. As soon as my back was turned to that room, I felt such an urge to run that I could hardly stand it. I forced myself to walk to the open door. I heard footsteps behind me, and I just hoped they were Norton's. When I got outside the building, I started to run. I dodged around to the front and raced along the gravel path. There was a shout of some kind behind me; I couldn't tell if it was "Help" or what. I took a quick look over my shoulder and saw Norton coming. Then I ran full tilt, with Norton pounding along behind me, going "Hnnmp" each time his foot hit the ground. When we reached the fence, I grabbed at the diamond spaces any old way and clawed my way up. As I was swinging over the top, I looked back to where we'd come from. I saw a swarm of pinprick yellow-green lights, but then I wasn't sure. The fence shook as we both scrambled down it.

We dropped to the ground on the other side, grabbed our bikes, and began to run pell-mell down the mountain, pushing the bikes in front of us. We slipped and stumbled, but we didn't stop running till we came to the chained entrance. We didn't unfasten the chain, but just shoved our way, bikes and all, through the bushes around it. Once we were standing on the dirt turnoff by the PRIVATE sign, I started to feel normal again.

"You know what happened?" Norton said between gasps for air. "Those bugs came after me. They came through the jar, right through the glass."

I didn't know what to say to that.

"Did your uncle see the jar when you were up here?" I asked.

"We didn't actually go into that building. We only looked around a little bit before he started setting up his telescope."

"Was that her car in the barn?" I said out of the blue.

"You mean she's got to be up there, don't you," said Norton, like a statement, not a question.

"That's what I've been thinking," I said, though, truth to tell, I hadn't thought it till that very second. "Didn't it seem like someone was watching us? I kept having this feeling that we were supposed to leave."

I was breathing easier by now, and my heart was no longer pounding. Standing next to Norton, I was suddenly aware of his stubby, friendly fingers—you know how you can be going along not paying attention and then you suddenly notice something that's been right beside you all the time?—and the way his collar stuck out of his sweatshirt and his sneaker toe spinning the pedal of his bike in a rhythm. I shoved my hands into my pockets. It was peaceful standing next to him. I felt safer with him there.

"Well, we could always ask her on Monday," I said. "See what she says."

"Monday we'll be going crazy with the game," said Norton.

"By the way, I have your card," I told him.

He gave me a crooked grin. "That's good. That means I'm safe unless you get caught."

"But who has mine?"

"I haven't heard anyone say."

"Did you know Amy got caught by Christina?" I said.

"She's not the only one," Norton said.

"Rachel and I went to see her. I was going to tell her about the sparks, but she was too sick to listen."

"She was sick?"

"Yeah—some virus thing. She was in bed. But she had made up her mind she was coming back to school on Monday."

"Some other kids came down with something over the weekend—that's what my mom heard. She kept asking me if I felt all right."

"So do you?"

"Yes! *I feel fine!*"

"Me too."

"I wish I could talk this over with Uncle Arthur."

"Maybe he knows more about why Fern Ridge closed."

By now, though, I was getting a feeling I knew why it had closed. "You know, we could ask Mr.

O'Hara. He might know about old schools. He knows all kinds of things. We could find him and ask him on Monday."

"I wonder who has Christina's card," said Norton.

I couldn't do anything but shrug my shoulders.

We rode away without any more talk.

When I got home I put my bike away in the garage and climbed the stairs to my room. My parents were still at the movie. I stood to one side of my window and pulled back the edge of the shade. Backyard dark. No fireflies. Full moon, very full moon. It was almost too bright. It seemed a little strange that I hadn't noticed it before, when we were outside. Had it been shining then? I let go of the shade. I could hear the drumbeats again, louder now; they had merged with the sound of my heart beating in my ears. I turned on all the lights in my room and left them on. I turned on the hall light and left it on. Then I went downstairs and watched television steadily until my parents came back.

"How are we doing?" asked my father.

"What're you watching?" my mother added.

They both gave me looks that brimmed with unspoken questions: Was I sick? Was I still seeing things?

I yawned conspicuously. "All quiet on the western front," I said. "G'night." I went upstairs. By then, strangely, the moon was gone; night was night again. It was comfortably dark outside my window, and I knew there was nothing alive in the yard except the usual—birds, squirrels, trees. I slept without waking until morning.

CHAPTER TEN

Every Sunday my parents divide up the newspaper—fat and smelling pleasantly of ink—and spend all morning reading it. They stay in their bathrobes and drink coffee and spread cream cheese on toasted bagels.

This particular Sunday morning I tried to nibble some cinnamon toast, but I didn't feel like eating. I helped clear away the breakfast dishes and followed my parents into the living room. I read the comics and Ann Landers and "Ask Beth," and then I figured it was late enough to make a phone call. I went up to my room and dialed Norton's number.

"Can you come over?" I asked. "Are you doing anything?"

"I can come around, sure," Norton said.

"Want to go to the library? It's open on Sunday afternoons. We could ask the librarian if they still have old newspapers and whatever. I want to find out what happened up there at Fern Ridge."

Norton came in time for lunch—I fixed us hot dogs and lemonade—and then we rode over to the library. I told Miss Turnbull, the librarian at the reference desk, that we wanted to do some research on Fern Ridge School, especially when it closed, and did she happen to know why?

"Every now and then people do get interested in that school," she said. "Someone came around here a couple of years ago asking that. Fellow teaching at your school. There's a bit of a mystery attached to it. You do your research first, and then I'll tell you what I know. But I'll tell you this right now: There's nothing much in the official town records. I tried to help that other party with this same subject. You can look in the newspaper files—we have them on microfilm—and I think there's an index to school accreditations in the state, the ones that were granted and then whether they were renewed or not. You'll find the year of its closure there." She scurried away to a shelf of large, dreary black books, picked out one, and handed it to Norton. We opened it on a table and leafed through it. We found the date without any trouble—1951—and then Miss Turnbull had us sit down at the microfilm machine and flip through editions of the *North Point Gazette* till we came to June 1951:

> *Fern Ridge School, an exclusive boarding school for boys, announced this afternoon that it was permanently closing its doors. Citing financial losses owing to a mysterious illness that swept through the school two years ago, officials said that enrollment was no longer sufficient to support the school, nor was it expected to rise. There are no plans at present for disposition of the buildings, although discussions are scheduled with the state for its possible use as a camp.*

"So what was the illness?" Norton asked.

"I haven't the foggiest idea," said Miss Turnbull. "I suppose some sort of Asian flu. You could try to find the state public health records for that year, if you want to take the time. It might mean several days of research. But listen, I have a better idea. There is a woman in town who used to teach at Fern Ridge. She's very old now, as you can imagine, probably ninety, and she lives in a nursing home. But she might remember. Let me give you her name. My sister works at the home—it's called Pine Meadows. She'll help you. I bet Miss Melrose would be thrilled to have visitors. Penelope Melrose is her name. And here is the address. It's only a few blocks from here. It's a very nice facility. Some of the more able-bodied residents even come here to the library and check out books."

I had never been in a nursing home, and when we first went through the wide entrance doors and a medicinal smell filled my nose, I wasn't sure this was going to be worth it. An attendant in a blue smock pushed a very old person by us in a wheelchair—the person was slumped to one side and his or her (you couldn't really tell which) eyes were closed. Then a really lively little lady, all dressed up in a black dress and with rouge on her cheeks and lots of blue eye shadow, came scampering up and said she'd been at this hotel all day and she was ready to go home now and asked us if that was what we were there for.

Norton, thank goodness, figured out what to say. "We only have our bikes," he told her, shaking his head.

"Oh, your bikes," she repeated. "I don't ride a bike." She darted over to a gentleman in a dark suit and bedroom slippers and told him she'd been at this hotel all day and asked if he was there to take her home.

Miss Turnbull's sister, who wore a name tag that said ELEANOR TURNBULL, came out from behind the receptionist's desk.

"My sister telephoned and said you were coming. I understand you'd like to visit Miss Melrose. She'll be so delighted. She has no relatives close by—I'm sure she gets lonely, though we try to keep all of our residents busy. She's a bit forgetful, but quite sharp, really, for someone her age."

We followed Miss Turnbull down a hall past nurses' stations and a glassed-in room in which a large group of white-haired people were placed in front of a television set. Some of them looked up at us mournfully (I thought) as we went by.

Miss Turnbull knocked on the door of room 106. Then she opened the door a crack. "Miss Melrose? The visitors I told you about are here. Are you ready to see them?"

"Yes indeed, yes indeed." The door opened farther, and a tiny woman with a bloom of white hair greeted us. She was wearing a flowered dress and a blue cardigan and running shoes. "Please come in." We stepped into a narrow room that held a bed, an ornate dresser, a nightstand, and one straight chair with a vinyl seat. The walls were full of photographs.

"How do you like my shoes?" she said. "They keep me fit." I noticed that her head kept faintly wobbling. Miss Turnbull had vanished and reappeared with a second chair, which she squeezed in next to the dresser. Then she left the room.

"Miss Turnbull says you want to know about my school," said Miss Melrose. "Now, where do you go to school?"

"We go to Oak Hill," said Norton.

"Is that boarding?"

"Nope. Day."

"Ah. My school is a boarding school—very different environment, you know. It's closed. It closed down. Did you know that?"

"That's what we were wondering about," said Norton.

"What happened?" I said. "Why did it close?"

"It's closed now, did you know? A tragedy, really. All the children were taken sick. No one knew what it was. All of them, and the other teacher, too, but I was not. It was all the ones who were staying over for the vacation, only six in all, and they were playing, you see."

"They were playing?" asked Norton.

"Yes. I was away, though, the day of the drawing. And the new boy—such a striking child. I can remember his face as if it were yesterday, more easily than I can remember what's her name who lives in the next room here. He was bright, too, caught on so quickly. He moved in right before the spring holidays. And then all of them, sick as dogs—some fever took their minds, and they raced out on a

130

moonlit night and were carried off! I saw it! Of course, no one believed me. They put me in a hospital for a while and said I must have gone sick in the head, too. So then I stopped talking about it, and I pretended I'd forgotten. I do still get mixed up about everyday things, you know. But I saw that. I was an eyewitness.

"But no one believed me. They had to say the children had gone off with the other teacher, Mr. Jackson. They said he kidnapped them, and the boys were never seen again. And neither was he. What a scandal. Police investigations, dogs searching for clues, you've no idea. And all the while I knew they were gone, gone, gone into the sky. And the beautiful boy was gone, too. Of course, no one would send their children back to Fern Ridge after that. It was in the national papers, though the school tried to keep it quiet. You can't keep a thing like that quiet. It was even in a national magazine. I used to have the clippings. Maybe I still do. Let me look."

Miss Melrose slowly slid off her perch on the end of her bed and stepped across to her bureau and opened the top drawer. There was an explosion of compressed socks and scarves and crocheted shawls. She rummaged around with a quaking hand and fished out a yellowed envelope. "Is this it?" She took out a clipping and handed it to me.

"'Nancy Conrad Marries,'" I read aloud. "I don't think so." I handed it back.

"Well, then, they've taken it," said Miss Melrose. "Like everything, lost. It was a wonderful school. I was a teacher in training; I was going to teach English. What a tragedy. Did I tell you it closed? The school had to close?"

After a bit, Norton and I thanked her and said we had to go home. "Can we ask you just one other thing?" Norton said. "You don't remember what they were playing on that school vacation, do you?"

"Oh, no, I was gone when they drew, so I didn't play. It's closed now, you know." She stood in the doorway as we left, as if there were something more she wanted to say but she no longer knew what it was—or even if there was something after all.

Norton and I stood in the nursing home lobby. "Did you believe her about the kids getting carried off?" I asked.

Norton nodded. "She's old and all, but that sounded like it really happened."

"We've got to tell somebody," I said.

He stared at the end of a sofa, looking a little sick. I knew he was thinking about his uncle.

"Let's go see Mr. O'Hara today, right now," I said. "I was going to ask him about this stuff on Monday anyhow. Do you know where he lives?"

"Let me call home. My mom might know. She did this volunteer thing at school, and I think she's got a teachers' phone list." Norton went over to the pay phone and put in a coin, and in a minute he came back with an answer: "Sixteen Cedarwood Terrace."

"Where's that?"

"It's one of those new places, out on the other side of the library, near Houghton's Pond."

"We could get there on our bikes," I said.

We picked our way through traffic across town.

Cedarwood Terrace turned out to be a group of brick town houses clustered around an open green space. There was a set of metal swings in one corner of the green space and a sandbox with a couple of cracked plastic toys. Number 16 was toward the end of the farthest building. We parked our bikes on the sidewalk that led up to the front door, and I rang the bell.

Mr. O'Hara answered right away. At first he looked somehow different, and I had the funniest feeling that his teacher's face was only an expression he put on, and not really his. "This is an unexpected pleasure!" he said. "Come in." He closed the door behind us. I couldn't help looking around for a minute, I was so surprised at his apartment. There was hardly any furniture, only an old orange couch in the corner with a spindly coffee table in front of it. Through an archway I got a glimpse of the kitchen. A light shone down on the kitchen table, where Mr. O'Hara's briefcase sat open, with our class's English papers spilling out. The apartment seemed bleak. I couldn't see any signs of food or cooking or any creature comforts at all.

"Do you have somewhere to eat supper?" I asked. "I mean, this place doesn't look very homey."

"I go to restaurants. Now, what's up?"

I noticed a wallet-sized photo tacked to the bulletin board over the sink. It was the same girl and the same picture as the one in his desk at school. "Well," I began, "first of all, I had a strange thing happen with Christina. On Friday after school got out, when there was nobody else around, I saw her sort of...dematerialize, I guess you could call it. She turned into sparks for a few seconds. Though I might have been seeing things. My parents think I was having a hallucination."

Mr. O'Hara turned away and began gathering up the papers and patting them into order. "I'm listening," he said.

"Well, so what do you think of that?"

"It must have been a pretty frightening experience."

"You're not kidding," I said.

"I'm not sure what to make of it. A number of people at school have gotten sick, and this could be another form of the flu."

"And also she could be an alien, couldn't she?"

Mr. O'Hara gave a thoughtful shrug. "Anything is possible," he said.

"Well, guess what else. Norton saw where she goes at night."

"I followed her car, and she went up to the top of Chickatawbut Hill," Norton said. Together we told Mr. O'Hara about our excursion and about seeing the car hidden in the shed. And then we repeated Miss Melrose's tale about Fern Ridge. "See, she said they were playing," Norton insisted. "She couldn't say what, but she said there was a drawing. It could be our same game."

"These games, or variations on them, are very old—they go back for generations," said Mr. O'Hara. "They're popular, and then they die out, but never entirely. Then someone starts it again. How good did you think this lady's memory was?"

"Pretty good," I said.

"Not so good," Norton said at the same time.

"Whatever happened, the kids got sick and the school closed. What if that's going to happen at Oak Hill?" I said.

Mr. O'Hara stayed frustratingly silent.

"Have you ever played?" asked Norton. "Wha
about at your old school?"

"Oh, well, *there...*," said Mr. O'Hara, which didn
answer the question. Then he patted his jacke
pocket. I remembered noticing him do that sam
thing on Friday, right after someone asked him abou
playing.

"What about her? Is that your daughter?" Nortor
stepped over to look at the picture on the bulletir
board. I sucked in my breath, because it was such
nosy question.

"Yes, that's my daughter." Mr. O'Hara's voic
sounded as if it had been squeezed thin.

The next question had to be where was she, an
even Norton had enough sense not to ask that. Nor
ton sighed. "Do you think we should get Mr. Bonne
to stop the game?"

"I doubt if he can," said Mr. O'Hara.

"Then the parents will get together and mak
the school stop it," I said.

"The game has already gone too far," said M
O'Hara. "Too many children have been captured
Once the game gets past the halfway point, it speed
up, and the rules start to slip. The children who'v
been caught have only one aim from that point on—
to keep the game going. Parents won't be able t

eep their children at home. The desire to return to he game becomes stronger the longer the game oes on. You can't keep them from it."

"You really do know a lot about it," said Norton autiously.

Right then I wanted to go home, no matter what Mr. O'Hara knew or didn't know. Mr. O'Hara eemed to want us to leave, too.

"If you ask me, the only thing to do is keep playng," he said. "I do mean that. If you ever take anyhing I say to heart, listen to this. Play as long as you an, right to the end."

He moved toward the door. "Say, whose cards o you two have?" he asked.

"Can't tell!" I said quickly.

Norton and I backed onto the stoop.

"Good night," said Mr. O'Hara. He closed the oor.

It was a grim ride back toward our houses. As we ot near the corner where Norton turns off, I said, You know, I was thinking—not that many kids have een caught yet. It's nowhere near half."

"Maybe we can still do something," said Norton. What about the teachers? Are any of them not laying?"

"We could find out on Monday. I know Miss righam really doesn't like the game."

CHAPTER ELEVEN

On Monday morning my mother must have felt my forehead ten times before I left for school, just to make sure I hadn't developed a fever. When my father stopped the car at the top of the hill, I waited to get out until I saw someone I knew to walk with. "I don't suppose there's any chance of you picking me up after school today?" I asked.

"I wish I could, dearie." Dad shook his head. "I've got faculty meetings till six. But you call me if you start to feel, you know, sick."

The only people coming along the path were a bunch of little boys, and after them two younger girls, running and giggling. Then the four Duckies came chattering down the path.

"Wait a sec!" I called to them. "See you, Dad."

caught up with them. "Mind if I walk with you?" I could tell they did.

"Sure, if you want to," said Claire.

"'S okay, if there's nobody you...," said Elizabeth.

"You don't happen to know, any of you, who has my card?" I asked.

"I thought I heard somebody say, but now I can't...," said Kiki.

"We can try to find out," said Claire.

"It's cool to play this year," said Tam. "So we might not tell you!"

"We wouldn't want to cheat," said Elizabeth, giggling.

"It's not cheating," I said.

"Who do you have?" Tam asked me.

"Norton."

"You could catch him without half-trying," said Elizabeth. They all laughed.

"Did you hear about the fake card?" said Kiki. "Someone got this card that said Anna Shreves, only there isn't any Anna Shreves. They're trying to find out who did it, because we can't do the drawing over. But somebody's making sure they can't get caught!"

A boy in our grade came pounding up behind us. "Gotcha!" he said, putting his hands around Kiki's waist.

"Not yet, Elliott," said Kiki, pushing him away. "You can't catch anybody now. You know that!"

"Duh, I forgot," said Elliott, pretending to play a dumb kid.

We kept on moving and pushed through the front doors of the school. Everyone was screaming even though the game couldn't start up again until the first class period was over. We went down the hall, past the painted wooden cubbies where the youngest children hang their jackets. This section of the school always smells a little bit like feet. When we turned the corner, I saw Christina at the far end of the next corridor, standing in the middle of a swirl of children, looking like the Pied Piper. I could see Marshall Flaherty right in the middle of them. Mrs. Kelly, a fourth-grade teacher, was watching Christina and smiling benevolently. I wondered if that meant Mrs. Kelly had been caught, too.

"Tomorrow at morning recess we're going to start a club! Let's meet at the bench by the gym," Christina was saying to the little kids. She looked across the tops of their heads and waved at us— probably she meant the wave only for the Duckies. "And when we all get together, I want you to tell me if you know about anybody who isn't playing. And meanwhile I'm going to ask Mr. Bonner if we all can

140

play, all of us, down to the youngest kids. Want to? Wouldn't that be fun?"

"See you," I said to the Duckies. I ran back through the kids milling around in the entranceway. Rachel was waiting for me by my locker. I twirled the lock, opened the door, and began getting my stuff in order for the morning. "Is Amy back in school?" I asked.

She nodded. "She looks fine, but she seemed kind of distant, like she didn't have anything to say to me."

"Wait till I tell you about where Norton and I went. Listen, Rachel, *don't get caught*. Be sure and don't let it happen."

Rachel shook back her hair. "Okay," she said, a question in her voice.

In homeroom everybody was restless. At first, Mr. O'Hara waited for the flurry to die down. Usually when he stood there silently waiting, that was enough. But today a scuffle broke out in back. Two kids in the front row leaned across the aisle and began to show each other their cards. Henry Semp drawled outright that he hadn't read the chapter.

"Who else has *not* done the homework?" Mr. O'Hara asked.

Homework? I couldn't even remember what it was.

Most people's hands went up.

"Some of us were sick over the weekend," said Dan Fields.

"I heard something was going around," said Mr. O'Hara. He turned to Henry. "Well, if you haven't read the chapter, what *have* you read?"

Henry shrugged and looked at his classmates in hopes of a sympathetic laugh.

"You must have read something since Friday."

"The sports page," he said finally.

"Tell us about it."

Henry turned red. His feet looked huge as he shuffled his sneakers back and forth beneath his chair.

"I don't remember," he said finally.

Mr. O'Hara folded his arms. "Has anyone here read anything at all?"

"I read something interesting in the newspaper," said Christina. "An article about aliens. Creatures from another galaxy."

I felt as if the air had just been squeezed out of my lungs.

"What about them?" said Mr. O'Hara.

"This woman thought one visited her. She saw

this lizard in her kitchen." Tittering laughs rippled through the class.

"Oh jeesh," said Dan with a snort.

"That's a lot of trash," said Henry.

"Not necessarily," said Kiki. "A lot of people have seen them."

"Yeah, and Elvis, too," said Henry.

"I'd love to find E.T. in my closet," said Elizabeth.

"Get a life, Duckworth," said Henry.

"Just because you can't explain it doesn't mean it isn't real," said Claire.

"Scientists know more than they're telling us," said Kiki.

"I met an alien once," said Christina. The room was instantly quiet. The Duckies nodded their heads to show they had heard this before. "I saw something giving off light in my backyard, like stars, and then a person came to my school and followed me, and it seemed as though she was taking thoughts right out of my head. It was when our school was playing the game, just like the game you play here. And so I played harder, because I was afraid of what would happen if I didn't win and this other person did. And I guess it worked, because here I am!"

"You must have been on something," said Henry sarcastically.

My ears were ringing. All the kids in class began asking questions: "What happened to the alien?" "Did she try to kidnap you?" "Is it still following you?"

"Sometimes I wonder!" Christina looked back at me. Everybody laughed.

"What do you say?" Henry asked Mr. O'Hara. "Do you believe in aliens?"

"I don't have a yes or no answer to that," said Mr. O'Hara.

By now we were all watching the clock, waiting for the bell. It rang, and everybody jumped up as if they had been shot from rubber bands. There was so much squealing and screaming, you couldn't tell who was getting caught and who was just making noise. The Duckies gathered up their notebooks and clustered around Christina, claiming her, keeping the other girls away. Rachel and I held on to each other, and Rachel grabbed Henry's wrist as we went on to math. By the time we got there, Christina's bundle of cards was visibly thicker.

I decided not to go out for recess at the end of math, and instead I went to look for Mr. O'Hara. He was in his office, at the back of the classroom. I saw that the photograph of his daughter was lying on his desk, partway out of the frame.

He looked up sharply when I came in. "Just trying to straighten this out," he said. He sounded flustered.

"She's really pretty." Now that I could see the picture up close, I could see how much she looked like him.

"Just an ordinary girl."

I tried to think of how to ask delicately what had happened to her. Recess didn't last long, and I couldn't stand not knowing. "Does she live around here? Do you ever see her?"

"She's...she's missing," he said. "There had been just the two of us. Her mother died some years ago."

"Your daughter didn't die, did she?"

He shook his head.

"You don't know where she is?"

"I still hope to find her. I can never give up until I do."

"What's her name?"

"Anna. Anna Shreves O'Hara."

"Oh." I scraped my toe along the floor. "Did you know a fake card turned up in the game? With almost that same name?"

I had a feeling Christina was going to dash by the window right then, her bright hair catching the sun, or materialize in Mr. O'Hara's office.

"I did hear about that, yes," Mr. O'Hara said.

Recess was over, so I left.

Rachel's and my last class before lunch was science. Miss Brigham placed three animal skeletons on the demonstration table. She had ordered them months before, she announced, and they had just come that morning: a raccoon, a mouse, and a cat. Next week we were going to study the bony structure of animals; we were so lucky we had these perfect specimens, because usually only colleges could afford them. "Would you please take your minds off that game and pay attention." Miss Brigham raised her voice a notch.

The skeletons were beautiful—each tiny white bone shaped for its function, all of them fitting together into a recognizable shape. But nobody took his or her mind off the game. Everyone watched the minute hand of the clock as it moved closer to 11:50, when class ended. I gripped the edges of my desk, ready to spring up and grab anyone's arm or leg I could get my hands on. Miss Brigham opened the glass doors of her science storage cabinet and began to put the skeletons away.

The bell rang: pandemonium.

I screamed and so did Rachel, and we latched onto each other. I looked around for Norton and saw him standing across the room by himself, scanning the mass of kids. Christina pushed through the mob toward the classroom door. She went up behind Elizabeth Duckworth and tapped her on the shoulder and showed her a card. "I knew it!" Elizabeth said, and stood there, looking up blindly at Christina. Christina drew a pencil mark across the card, collected the one Elizabeth had been holding, and gave her a quick hug around the shoulders. She whispered something to her, and both of them looked back at Rachel and me. Then they linked hands with a string of kids and began to tug the line toward me. Norton pushed through the room and grabbed my hand.

A horde of shrieking kids staggered in from the corridor—"Woops, sorry, Miss Brigham!" shouted one of them—and lurched backward and fell in a heap of bodies, knocking over chairs and several people.

Miss Brigham turned the lock in her cabinet door and called for order. "We should never have started this game! This is worse than any other year! I am going to take those cards away right now." She began to move from person to person, snapping cards out of their hands.

Several desks slid together as the herd pushed across the room. A howl of pain went up.

"Ow, ouch, my fingers!" wailed Kiki, starting to cry. Someone grabbed at her hand, and she crumpled up on that side and screamed.

Christina made her way toward Miss Brigham. "Isn't that against the rules, taking cards away, Miss Brigham? You aren't playing, are you?" she said.

"No, I'm not playing. I hate this game, and I'm going to tell Mr. Bonner to stop it. This is madness. We are supposed to have a school here." She bent down to look at Kiki's fingers.

I shook off a girl who had fastened onto my arm and was trying to pull herself up from the floor. I dragged Rachel and Norton with me. We were nearly out of the room when I saw a boy grab Miss Brigham's wrist and force the cards from her hand.

"Jeesh," said Norton. "Let's get out of here." We raced out of the room and down the hall to the lunchroom. We stopped at the doorway. Unwrapped sandwiches and bags of chips skidded across the Formica tables as kids from every grade flew at each other. Someone's cards fluttered to the floor, and a crowd landed on them like scavenging crows, snatching them up with cries and shouts.

"Wait a minute. Didn't you say you had Jennifer Akers's card?" I asked Norton. "Look." A knot of seventh graders was expanding and contracting like a swarm of bees near the lunchroom door, and I could see Jennifer clinging to its fringe. "Get ready," I said. I slipped away and went over to the girl next to Jennifer and grabbed at her wrist and squealed, "Save me! Save me! Norton's over there!" I made myself scream a lot while I held on to both of them, pretending I was running from Norton. Norton charged after us. We backed up against the wall, still screaming, and then I let go, and Norton tagged Jennifer.

"You said he was after you," Jennifer said crossly. "You'll never get anywhere with that card," she added to Norton. Norton looked at it and tucked it underneath his other cards.

"Who?" I asked.

"Find a table," he said.

"Hey, where's Rachel?" I looked around. Christina and Elizabeth were talking to Rachel at the lunchroom door. "Rachel!" I yelled, and I waved and jumped up and down. I didn't think she had been caught. "Come sit with us!" She started walking toward us. "You haven't been caught, have you?" I asked her. She shook her head.

We found places at the table where Amy was already sitting. Henry and Dan were at the other end, and two more boys came up and got into seats by climbing over the chair backs.

At that moment a hush fell over the lunchroom.

At every table, a couple of people or more sat as if they had been flash-frozen. Kids had their mouths hanging open, looking up or down, reaching for a paper napkin, and they all had the same blank look on their faces: Their bodies were present, but the rest of them was not. It looked to me as if their eyes had a faint frosty coating. Dan had turned into a lump of lead, his face as heavy as a sandbag. He sat with his lips pursed about an inch above the end of his straw.

"Dan?" I tapped him on the arm.

I looked at Norton, who was making an incredible racket with his waxed paper. Then I noticed Amy. She gazed off as if she was dreaming, her hands poised over her can of soda, the tab partly lifted up.

"Hey, what's going on?" said Henry, looking around.

The moment passed. The room buzzed again. Amy rubbed her temples and shook her head.

"Hey, man, you okay?" Henry took Dan's elbow with awkward concern.

"What happened to you just now?" I asked Amy.

"I don't know." She rubbed her forehead. "It felt like when I was sick over the weekend."

"Did you see all these other kids—," I began.

"For God's sake, Zoe, leave me be, okay? You're

so worried, so nosy. The game this, the game that. I love playing the game. And frankly, sitting next to you all the time blows my mind. And sitting next to Norton blows my appetite."

Norton looked surprised, his sandwich drooping halfway to his mouth.

"At least you guys are playing," Amy went on. "The people that aren't—something's going to happen to them."

She stood up and pushed back her chair, scooped up her lunch, tossed it in the trash can, and walked off.

"She never talks like that," said Henry. "I've never ever heard her say stuff like that."

"You ought to try listening," said Dan.

"But she's not like that," said Henry. Then he looked twice at Dan. "What'd you say?"

"See you later, fathead. That's what I say." Dan left the table.

"What?" said Henry.

Norton put his hand on my arm and whispered, "Zoe, Zoe, listen. I got her card. I got Christina's."

CHAPTER TWELVE

The game went on like that, with everyone in a frenzy, the rest of the day. I would say that at least half the kids in school were caught by the end of lunch recess, and even more by the time the last bell rang. When I came out of French, everyone was dragging through the halls, looking exhausted, and a lot of them were complaining about not feeling well. Most kids went straight to their lockers and packed up and started for home without even talking to each other.

Norton and Rachel and I had agreed to meet after school and talk for a minute before Rachel's mother picked her up. Norton was waiting by the front door, his bike leaning against the brick wall. We watched people come out of the school—

nobody horsing around or yelling rude jokes at each other or joining up to go to the mall on their way home. When Rachel came out, her face looked gray. I tried to meet her eyes, but she kept looking away. The three of us walked up the path.

"Rachel?" I said. I didn't need to ask her outright.

She nodded. "It was only Vicki Saunders. She got me at the end of French. But I feel awful. I'm going home to lie down." Mrs. Flaherty's van was parked at the top of the hill. Someone else's mother was leaning on the driver's side door and talking to her through the open window. Both mothers turned when they saw Rachel. Mrs. Flaherty reached across and opened the passenger door. Rachel slid in without a word. Mrs. Flaherty and her friend looked at Rachel for a moment.

I went around to the driver's side window. "She doesn't feel good," I said to Mrs. Flaherty. "Half the school is sick. Something is really wrong."

"So I gather," said Rachel's mother. "Amy was sick over the weekend, wasn't she? Though she got over it in forty-eight hours or so. I wonder if this is some kind of epidemic. How about you two?" Norton had come up beside me.

"We're okay," said Norton.

"I think we'll have a word with Mr. Bonner," said Mrs. Flaherty. "Do you need a lift?"

"No thanks, we're walking," I said.

Norton pushed his bike, and we started toward my house. "So Christina must have caught Vicki Saunders after Vicki caught Rachel!" Norton said. "Otherwise, Rachel wouldn't be acting sick."

"How'd she have time?" I asked.

"She's fast," muttered Norton.

"I still can't figure out who has my card," I said. "Nobody's even tried to catch me. But I found out one thing—that fake card? It's got Mr. O'Hara's daughter's name on it."

"I hope that isn't somebody's idea of a joke," said Norton.

"Why can't we at least *try* to get Mr. Bonner to stop the game?" I said. "He's the director of the school; he can decide to cancel the whole thing if he wants to. Except—wait a second—if Rachel's caught, and she had Mr. Bonner's card, that means Christina has to go after Mr. Bonner next."

We both turned around to look at the school in the distance, as if we could actually check on Mr. Bonner from there. Norton shook his head. "Can't do anything about her," he said.

"You could tag her," I said.

"Then you could tag me," he said.

"I don't want her card."

"You think I do?"

After six or seven blocks, Norton got on his bike and rode off toward his house. "I'm going to visit my uncle. Call me tonight," he yelled back.

I walked on toward my street. At first I didn't hear anything. Then the sound of a smoothly running engine was beside me, and the black car was there, following me at my exact pace. It stopped, and the door opened and Christina beckoned to me from the front seat. "Want a ride?" I froze. The inside of the car was dark, and I had an impression of leather seats and luxury. But what really got me was that there was no driver. "Come on! It'll only take a minute." She beamed her catalog smile.

"I'm walking," I said.

"Want to go to the mall?"

"No thanks."

"Then I'll walk with you." She hopped out, and the car stopped. The door closed behind her on its own. We stood facing each other on the sidewalk, in front of the Hatfields' house. Mrs. Hatfield was digging around a shrub in the yard, and she kept looking over at us to see what we were up to.

"Who are you, anyway?" I asked. My knees were full of accordion pleats.

Christina stood solidly planted on her long, perfect legs. "You know me pretty well, don't you?"

"I know you're good at the game," I said. "You've

caught my two best friends, haven't you?" I took a deep breath to cover up my shaking voice.

"I've had plenty of practice. That's the only reason I came."

"Where from?" I choked out.

"Nowhere in particular. My family are wanderers, like circus families. We follow the game. It's always being played somewhere in the universe."

She took a couple of steps toward me, and I was afraid she was going to try to tag me. If she'd captured Mr. Bonner, and he'd had my card, she'd be after me. That could explain why nobody had heard of anyone with my card. Mr. Bonner wasn't going to run around sharing information.

I moved back till I was standing on Mrs. Hatfield's lawn. I knew Mrs. Hatfield would notice that, because she hates having anyone step on her grass. "Mr. O'Hara says they played it at his old school," I said. "And they probably played it at Fern Ridge, too."

"Yes. Those were complete games. All the cards were captured, or nearly all, anyway—enough to finish the game. Looks like this game is going to be a complete one, too. You might even win it."

"I don't want to win!" I said.

"I think you do. Because you know something, don't you? Don't you have a secret? You've hidden the card with your name on it, haven't you?"

"I don't have it," I said truthfully.

"Who does?"

"I don't know." Now I was sure she didn't.

Christina's eyes glittered. "Someone will win this game. It's nearly complete, and there's no undoing it. You would be a fine winner. I picked you out myself." She took a couple of steps toward me, and as she got very close, she turned to a mass of swirling pinprick lights that swarmed right in my face. Mrs. Hatfield was still busy digging. "Get away from me!" I shouted. Mrs. Hatfield dropped her shovel with a clatter and looked up. I started to run and I kept running and I didn't look back. A few seconds later the black car shot past me and drove out of sight. I kept hearing Christina's words in my head: *I picked you out myself, I picked you out myself.* I ran four more blocks and up our front steps and into our living room. "Mom! Mom!" My voice sounded terrified, even to me.

CHAPTER THIRTEEN

My mother was on the telephone, but I heard her drop it and run out to me. "What is it? Zoe, what's the matter?"

"I just saw the most horrible thing! Christina—that girl I said was an alien—she just sort of exploded right in my face. Ask Mrs. Hatfield! I was in front of her house, and Christina came up in that black car and tried to get me to go in it, only I wouldn't. Then she threatened me; she said I was going to win the game!"

My mother's face had a mixed expression—partly afraid, partly not believing what I was telling her. I was guessing she was going to get mad. She's not good at taking things on faith and figuring them out slowly. If it scares her or can't be explained, she wants to get rid of it right then.

"Zoe, you are hysterical!" she said. That was hardly news. "I was just on the phone with Meg Flaherty. There's definitely something going around the school, some disease, and playing this game has made it worse. She and some other parents are going to call Mr. Bonner and ask him to put a stop to the game. She's also taken Rachel to the doctor."

"It might already be too late for Mr. Bonner. Christina is the one you ought to be taking to a doctor. Or jail or something! Can't you find someone who knows how to get rid of aliens? What about the people who get rid of termites and things?"

"I'm going to keep you at home," said my mother crisply. "Fever or no, you're not all right. And furthermore, I think your father should come home early." She called him at his office, and he did. By the time he had driven up, the telephone had rung three more times. I heard my mother say, "Yes, I've been hearing about that. It's time for the parents to do something. Maybe some of us should go over there tomorrow. We'll try telephoning tonight; perhaps we can arrange a meeting first thing with Mr. Bonner." She said more or less the same thing to the other two people who called.

"Surely Bonner can handle the situation at school. That's his job, isn't it?" I heard my father tell my mother. "How could he let things get to such a pitch?"

I went out to the kitchen to have some juice and try to collect myself. Someone had to have my card. I wondered if Mr. O'Hara knew, even though he wasn't playing. But why wouldn't he have told me if he did? Maybe it had somehow gotten lost, dropped in one of those hysterical crushes of kids, kicked under a bookshelf. I began to think that was my best hope—that it was lost and would stay lost.

During the rest of that afternoon and most of the evening, my parents talked to other parents. The Oak Hill kids all had the same symptoms: They didn't feel good, went to bed as soon as they got home from school, had no appetite, but were absolutely determined to go to school the next day. Nothing would have kept them at home. "Rachel's a maniac on the subject," said Meg Flaherty, according to my mother.

I didn't feel like eating much supper, and I went up to my room early and lay on my bed. My mother kept coming upstairs to check on me.

The phone was too busy for me to call Norton. Finally a group of parents made a plan to go into Oak Hill in the morning and sit down with Mr. Bonner and make it clear that he had to stop the game. My father was going to be one of them. That did make me feel better. Dad is slow to catch on to things sometimes, but once he gets going, he keeps after it. My mother would rather stay home, have him go out as deputy, and wait to hear what happened.

I didn't sleep very well. I kept jerking awake and pulling my shade back a sliver and looking out, afraid I would see the sparks, but even more afraid of having Christina out there with me not knowing it. Somehow, I thought everything would be all right if I could just make it to the next day.

The next morning, Dad and I left the house at the usual time. My mother wanted me to stay home, but I talked her out of it when I reminded her that Rachel's mother was letting her go. "Be sure and call me after you've been to school," my mother called out to Dad. "And, Zoe, if one more odd thing happens, you are to come home—don't even ask, just leave."

"We'll go over there and have a look-see," said my father. He cleared his throat several times, and we got into the car. He drove along, humming. He always hums when he's nervous but doesn't want to show it. He doesn't care for confrontations.

When we got to school, we parked, and Dad walked down the path with me. Several other parents were arriving with their kids, too, so it wasn't as embarrassing as it could have been. They all had the same looks on their faces: *I'm not used to being here, either, and I knew something was up.*

"Now we're going straight to Mr. Bonner's office and see what's what," said my dad.

Lots of other parents had gathered in the front hall, looking nervous. None of the other kids waited with the parents, but I hung around for a few more minutes.

Mrs. Webster greeted everyone cheerfully. "Did you have an appointment? Mr. Bonner is tied up with meetings most of the morning, and Miss Albrecht has to teach a class for a teacher who's absent."

Mr. Bonner came out of his office. "Any more coffee?" he asked Mrs. Webster. I could see through his open office door that there weren't any people already meeting there.

"Mr. Bonner—about this game the children are playing," began one father, stepping forward. "There's an unhealthy atmosphere being created at the school, a kind of group hysteria, and my wife and I wanted to suggest—"

"Oh, it's nothing, nothing!" Mr. Bonner laughed.

"Just enthusiastic players. We love the game—it's an old tradition, and we wouldn't dream of giving it up, not now, when we're over halfway through!" He hesitated in his doorway. "I can give you a few minutes, if you like."

My dad hummed a few bars to himself and spoke up. "Has anyone from the board of trustees called you yet?"

"Not that I know of," said Mr. Bonner. I saw him exchange a glance with Mrs. Webster.

"The issue is one of control," said my father.

But now all the kids, especially the captured ones, were acting perfectly well behaved. They walked by in twos and threes, their books held neatly under their bent arms, chatting quietly. "Good morning, Mr. Bonner!" Dan Fields called in a voice so cheery it made me wince.

Some of the parents turned to each other and discussed what to do. A few of them volunteered to go in and speak with Mr. Bonner at length and let the other ones know what was decided.

My father said he had better go on to his school, and he didn't feel uneasy leaving me, because the situation was far from the emergency he had imagined.

"Can't you stay a while longer?" I whispered to him. "Don't go yet. They're not acting like themselves. Now they're being too good."

"You have my phone number, and you can let me know if you need me. Just leave class if you have to. I promised I'd chair a meeting at school. Things look calm, dearie."

When I got to my desk in homeroom, everybody else was already there. I tapped Rachel on the shoulder. She turned partway and shook her head, and I knew from the gray color of her skin that she was gone.

Class began, but I don't think you'd really have called it school. Of course nobody had done any homework; Mr. O'Hara decided to read to us, and he barely managed to keep us quiet. No one listened. When we changed classes at the end of English, I saw the delegation of parents leave the school.

When Norton and I went out for morning recess, we looked for the "club" of little kids Christina had collected. They were crowded around the bench that stood to one side of the gym entrance. Christina was standing in their midst. We hung around the back. Some boys on the fringes of the group were fidgeting and wrestling with each other.

"Is everybody here playing the game?" Christina asked.

They nodded; they yawned; there was a chorus of "Ya-a-as."

"Good! We used to play this game at my old school, and it was so much fun, just like here!"

A couple of children clapped.

"Is there anybody not playing?"

The children looked at each other as if to find the answer. "No!" they began to shout back.

"I know that someone isn't playing," said Christina. "Does anyone know who it is?"

"My mother!"

"You!"

"Mr. Bonner."

"Nope." Christina shook her head. "It is a grown-up, though, I'm pretty sure. And I think everyone should play, don't you?"

"Everybody!" More hands clapped.

"If we're going to play together, then we should all be included. That's what the game is for—to help us get to know each other, and if even one person doesn't play, then that is spoiled. I think we should teach this person a lesson—even if it's the kids teaching the teacher. If we all banded together, we could talk her into playing, or make her play, couldn't we?"

There was a silence. A jet droned far overhead

and some branches rustled in the tantalizing breeze. Full, fragrant spring was gentle all around us.

"How could we make her?" asked a boy. "I mean if it's a teacher. We can't do that."

"Sure we can. If we had to, we could. There are lots of us, and only one of her."

"I don't think so." One little girl shook her head.

"Oh yes," said Christina with a confident nod.

"The game, the game, that's all we care about," cried a little boy, stamping his feet. "The game, the game!"

The other children joined in the chant, and it spread until everyone was shouting it as a cheer.

"It's time to go in," said Christina. "Now remember, we want everyone to play. Whoever doesn't play—we have to get rid of them. Let's meet before lunch by the gym door."

The children wandered off, and Christina went into the school.

Norton and I went down to the gym door at the end of the morning. I thought of calling my dad, but I didn't want to bother him unless I was sure something was really going to happen. A crowd of kids was waiting for Christina. She pushed her way through them and began telling them something, I couldn't hear what. The children turned and started toward us, then moved on past. They were chattering among themselves in odd, high-pitched voices, and their eyes had a whitish glaze.

They trooped down the first-floor hallway and around the corner, along the lines of gray lockers toward the science room. We followed them at a distance. The laboratory door stood open. Miss Brigham was in her office at the back, and she peeked out cheerfully when she first heard them. "Hello?"

Christina walked over to the cabinet and pointed to the animal skeletons. "Let's get them out," she said.

A murmur of yesses swept through the group.

"What?" Miss Brigham came out of her office.

"Try the door," said Christina.

The children clustered in front of the cabinet, and one girl reached up and tried to turn the knob. The door was locked, so she tugged at it and gave it a kick. Miss Brigham began to push her way through the mass of children toward the front of the room. "Stop that!" she cried. Another child reached up and pulled on the brass knob until the cabinet frame shivered and the glass gave a rattling sound. The knob came off. A thin laugh spread through the group.

Miss Brigham shoved past two children as she

reached for the cabinet, and the children tripped over each other and fell down. Immediately the entire pack closed in on Miss Brigham, giving out a chattering sound, like a lot of monkeys. They backed her up against the glass cabinet front and pressed against her harder and harder until the glass shattered with an explosive crack. She fell backward, then caught herself on the wood frame, jumped to one side, and stood, gasping, by the lab tables. Glass lay broken in hundreds of tiny pieces everywhere. The children turned and poured out of the room, their chattering sound reaching a shrill, deafening peak. Christina reached through the broken door and took out the three skeletons. She dropped them on the floor, crushed them under her foot, and left the room.

"We've got to get some help!" I said to Norton. Miss Brigham hung on to the table with one trembling hand.

"I need to sit down," she said.

"Are you all right?" I helped her across the mass of broken glass to a chair.

"I'm not cut badly, I don't think." She examined her hands and arms; there were some small cuts, and drops of blood began to well up. "I'm all right. The cabinet has safety glass, thank goodness. This is a matter for the police. I don't know what's gotten into the director this past day or two, but he's let the school run wild. He wouldn't listen to anything I said. I'm going home. I'm going to call the police myself."

Norton ran back in. "Mr. Bonner won't come. He's too busy. All Mrs. Webster says is, 'Can't it wait till school is out?' And I looked for Mr. O'Hara, but he's not in his office."

"This is a matter for the police," Miss Brigham repeated. She gathered up her purse and coat and disappeared down the hall, leaving the science room in chaos behind her.

CHAPTER FOURTEEN

Norton and I came out with extreme caution. We could hear wild voices in the lunchroom, storms of sound rising louder and louder, and then abrupt silence. All I could think of was that I wanted to get to the pay phone and call my dad, but the phone was right across from Mrs. Webster's office, and I was afraid to try with her sitting right there. When we got to the lunchroom, we went around the edge, heading for the playground door. It seemed as if we'd be safer if we could just get outside.

Every seat at every table was taken, but no one was eating anything. Now no one was talking; scarcely anyone moved. Dan and Henry had their heads down on their arms, and their lunch bags sat beside their elbows, unopened. The trash cans were full of sandwiches, granola bars, apples. When Christina arrived, the room crackled with attention and murmuring rose from one corner. Then it died away. Norton and I waited out lunch on the playground. Still nobody had tried to tag me.

When we went back in, I walked as unobtrusively as I could up toward the front office, clutching some coins in my hand. They were slippery with sweat. As I got near the pay phone, I could feel Mrs. Webster's eyes on me. I looked in her direction, and she gave me a weird smile; her eyes were cold and opaque, just like the captured kids'. I went on by.

As the afternoon began, the whole school was silent. Kids lurched through the halls with their eyelids half-shut. In some classrooms, they went in, put their heads down on their desks, and slept, while the teachers sat back and looked out the windows.

At the beginning of social studies, Miss Brigham came by the classroom door with Mr. Bonner, Miss Albrecht, and two policemen. "Perfectly orderly now," Mr. Bonner was saying. In a few moments they came back and stepped into the room. "Excuse us!" Mr. Bonner said. "There was an unfortunate incident in the science laboratory this morning, and these police officers are here to help us investigate. Did anyone in this class witness the event?"

I didn't want to say I had. If I stood up and offered to help the police, I was sure I would be the next target.

"It seems to have been the younger children," said Mr. Bonner. "We've never had any experience like this, never in the history of the school." He sounded just like his usual self.

"They acted as if they had turned into something not human," said Miss Brigham to the policemen. "Their eyes were white. Christina Blake, a tall blond girl who's new, was leading them."

"We're so glad the police have come," Miss Albrecht said, pointedly ignoring Miss Brigham. "I don't think Miss Brigham is exaggerating about the attack, because the cabinet certainly is broken. But I wonder if we need a police presence. I think it would be wise for us to conduct our own investigation within the school, knowing we could turn to you for assistance if we needed it." The group left the room. Miss Albrecht had her usual calm, dignified manner; I knew she was trying above all else to get the policemen to leave.

At 3:15 the bell rang for the end of school. Instead of pouring into the hallways, everyone stayed at their desks, everyone except Norton and me. We left French together. The whole class watched us go without expression. Mr. LeBlanc appeared to be totally absorbed in his notes. "What's going on now?" I whispered. We went together to Norton's locker, then to mine. I was putting my things into my backpack when I heard the chattering sound again, coming from the classrooms. Kids began streaming out into the hall and past me, heading out of the building, toward the parking lot. Norton got shoved to the other side of the corridor.

I inched my way along the lockers to the science room, where a row of big windows overlooked the teachers' cars. From a door on the right I saw Mr. O'Hara emerge from the building and start across the asphalt. He stopped and looked about him, as if seeking an escape route, then headed straight on for his car. They began clawing at him as he struggled to open the driver's side door. They pulled him to the ground, but he managed to get back on his feet. Then so many children surrounded him that all I could see was the top of the car door hanging open. There was no shouting, only a methodical, silent pounding. The car rocked on its tires. Suddenly it lurched forward. Knots of children still swarmed over it, but it moved again, a few more feet, and by fits and starts crossed the parking lot. Finally it turned onto the street and drove away. I couldn't tell if Mr. O'Hara was behind the wheel or not.

By the time I had stepped out into the hall, the

mob of children had turned and was heading back into the school. I had no idea where Norton was; I hoped he'd been able to get out of the school altogether. I had to hide. I guessed they wouldn't come back to Mr. O'Hara's room, since they had dispensed with him. I ran down the hall and ducked into it as voices burst through the school doors. Feet trampled past. I crouched beneath Mr. O'Hara's desk. Minutes crawled by. The buzzing sound of voices faded away, worked up to a crescendo again, then finally dwindled to nothing. The silence stretched out to twenty minutes. At last I crept out from my cramped hiding place and tiptoed over to the door. The school was deserted, the back doors chained shut, as if no one was expected to return.

I slipped my backpack over my shoulders and wrenched open one of the windows in Mr. O'Hara's classroom. I dropped to the ground and started for home.

"Zoe! I've been so worried!" my mother scolded. "Norton has been calling. Apparently there was some terrible fight or something in the parking lot, and he was afraid you'd gotten caught in it."

"The kids went after Mr. O'Hara, and they attacked him in his car," I said, starting to cry.

"What do you mean, attacked?"

"I couldn't see very well, there were so many of them. They've all turned into crazy people."

"Zoe, sit down and take a deep breath."

"Will you take me over to Mr. O'Hara's? I'm afraid he's hurt."

"This doesn't sound like anything for you to get mixed up in."

"What if he needs a doctor? He lives all by himself. He might not even know a doctor."

"Zoe, he's a grown-up. I'm sure he can take care of himself."

"You could just drive up and wait. You don't have to come in with me."

"I knew I should have kept you at home! Where was Mr. Bonner?"

"He's no help. Remember I told you how Christina captures people in the Elimination game? She takes over people's minds once she catches them, and she can make them do what she wants. That's what this epidemic thing is that's going through the school. Besides the kids, she's got Mr. Bonner and Mrs. Webster and half the teachers or more. And this other school that played the game, well, the kids who played disappeared at the end of it. Now see what I was trying to tell you? I wasn't seeing things."

My father walked in then.

"Well, you're home early!" said my mother.

"This is quite a situation at Oak Hill," he said. "The president of the board apparently tried to talk to Bonner this afternoon, and they had a most unsatisfactory conversation. Now, when I was there this morning, it looked like a model school. But there was some kind of attack on a science teacher this morning."

"I wanted to call you, Dad, but I was scared to use the phone! Mrs. Webster was sitting there watching me with these horrible metal eyes."

"Listen to what Zoe says," said my mother. "The children turned into a mob after school, and they attacked Mr. O'Hara."

I described it all for my father. "Can we please just go see Mr. O'Hara and find out if he's okay? He knows a lot about the game, Dad. Maybe he can help us figure out how to stop it."

"How does he come to know about it? I always did wonder about that fellow—no connections anywhere," said my dad.

"He played it at his old school," I said. "Let's find him, Dad, *please.*"

So my father and I got into our car and drove to Mr. O'Hara's garden apartment. We went up to the front door, but it was clear no one was home. There were no lights on, and nobody answered the bell. I glanced at the parking lot behind the building; Mr. O'Hara's car wasn't there.

My mother had had more phone calls by the time we got back home. "There's another strange thing going around among the kids who are sick—a few of them have been sleepwalking. Yesterday, Amy Johnson's mother caught her standing outside in the dead of night in her pajamas. Anyway, there's a meeting tonight at the Flahertys'. They're going to organize the parents and station one in every classroom tomorrow, and they've asked for a special police detail. I think they should just close down the school."

"I'll go to the meeting," said my father. "I'm going to suggest that we declare an emergency and ask for an official from the Centers for Disease Control."

I ate a few bites of macaroni and cheese. The parents could meet all night, but it wouldn't make any difference, because they weren't playing the game. Only game players could do anything, and there wasn't much time left. The game was moving fast.

While I was sitting at the kitchen table, the front doorbell rang madly. Someone was just leaning on the bell. I ran to the door and saw Norton peering through the glass panels. I yanked open the door.

"I've been trying to call you for hours," Norton

practically shouted. "I've got to warn you. One of the kids in that attack on Mr. O'Hara came by my house. My mom really freaked when she saw her—it was Vicki Saunders, only with the pearly eyes and perfect manners. What she said was that they found out Mr. O'Hara was trying to wreck the game by putting in a fake card and hiding someone's real card. And the card he had was yours, Zoe. They took it from him. I guess that's what the attack was about. And now Christina's got it."

CHAPTER FIFTEEN

School began the next day with a parent stationed in every classroom. It turned out the classes didn't need monitors, though, because all the kids behaved perfectly—if you can call robots perfect. They were absolutely polite: If they couldn't answer a question, they apologized; when someone did know an answer, the others would blink their coated eyes and say, "Good thinking, Robert," or whoever.

A substitute was standing beside Mr. O'Hara's desk when we came into homeroom. I waited for her to make some announcement about Mr. O'Hara, but she didn't. None of the kids asked about him, either. "I am Mrs. Harris, and I will be your teacher today," was all she said.

I heard the parent monitors talking among themselves all day. The kids were supposedly behaving, but the parents could tell they were sick. A consultant from the Centers for Disease Control was flying in the next morning.

At morning recess two teams of boys and girls played basketball. Everybody else stood on the sidelines and cheered. Their voices were in perfect unison; everyone hit every basket; no one disputed anything. I should say *our* voices were in unison—Norton and I went along with the others, though we couldn't fake the coated eyes. The few kids Norton had captured, and the one I had tagged, Molly Frick, weren't at school. Their parents hadn't had any trouble keeping them at home.

All that day, wherever I looked, I saw Christina's swirl of silver hair and I heard Christina's light footsteps. But she completely ignored me. No one chased anyone anymore. Everybody seemed to turn away from me. The teachers droned on, and the kids sat in their places, rows of unresponsive heaps, and the parent monitors stood at the back of each classroom and waited for something wild to happen, but nothing did. It would almost have been better if there was some crazy outburst, I heard one of them say; it would have given them something to act on, instead of this endless waiting.

Then, toward the end of the day, everyone began whispering to each other. I couldn't make out the words, but the whispers spread from desk to desk, row to row, and then class to class.

None of the kids in the game would speak to me, or even seemed to know I existed, but still I tried. I tapped Henry on the arm. "What is everyone saying?" He pulled away from me. I hurried after Rachel on the way to French. "What are you whispering about?" She shook her head. I kept after her. "Tell me."

"It's only for us," she said.

"Tell me."

She looked away.

But the whispers went on: "Tonight, tonight." "Only for us." "Enough now." "Tonight on Chickatawbut Hill." Finally all the words came clear: "It will be finished tonight. On Chickatawbut Hill."

Norton and I stood together and watched everyone leave school at 3:30. Talk about the walking dead—they were gray-faced, stony-faced, and looked as limp and dragging as if they had been on a forced march for the past month.

"Something's happening on Chickatawbut tonight," I said.

"So what?" Norton said. "What if we just held out for weeks and weeks?"

"But we have to keep playing. That's the one thing Mr. O'Hara told us."

"Why should we do what he said?"

I bit my lip. "The thing is, his school played the game before."

I didn't have any appetite at supper, but I picked at my spaghetti and made myself swallow a few bites. My parents asked me a few questions about how school had gone.

I went up to my room and sat on my bed for a while. I kept seeing Mr. O'Hara, the way he had been standing helplessly by his car, clutching his shabby briefcase, and then all the children swarmed at him.

I wondered where he was now, alive or dead. Maybe he had escaped, if only barely, and had driven to some other state, somewhere far away. I couldn't think of a reason why he would have hidden my card all that time. And I couldn't see why he had put a fake card into the game, either. Unless he thought that if he put Anna's name on the card, that would call her back. Maybe he was going to go on searching for his daughter. Maybe he would look for another school that was going to play the game.

I wasn't giving up. I was going to do what Mr. O'Hara said and keep playing to the end. There was no one who had a chance of stopping the game except us, players who weren't caught yet.

At midnight I woke up. I hadn't meant to fall asleep. I was still in my clothes, but my parents must have come in, because somebody had pulled my quilt over me. I sat up and listened. The house was quiet. It was pitch-black outside. I had already decided I was not riding my bike to Chickatawbut. If nothing else, I wanted to be able to run to a car if I had to. I pulled on a sweatshirt and crept downstairs. Once I was outside, I closed the front door silently and sat down to pull on my sneakers and socks. I was going to walk the ten blocks to Rachel's and wake up Tim and get him to drive me and Norton. He'd said he knew how Saturday morning. I could talk him into it somehow. We'd drive to Norton's and sneak him out.

The streets and sidewalks were empty. New leaves like turning shadows rustled in the breeze. Then I saw someone coming toward me. My heart jumped like a frog. Carefully, without letting myself panic, I crossed to the other side of the street. It was a child; and there, a couple of blocks farther down, came another one, dressed in nightclothes, walking steadily toward me. They didn't seem to see me— they passed by and kept on walking. I turned and watched them vanish in the shadows, reappear beneath a streetlight, then be swallowed up again. They were walking south, in the direction of Chickatawbut Hill.

I hurried. Another kid, a small one in shorty pajamas, maybe six years old, came out of a side porch and went up the sidewalk. I thought I heard him whispering to himself, a gentle, sighing whisper that went past my ears like a dying breath. He looked too young to have played the game from the beginning; he must be one of the very young ones Christina had brought in toward the end. As I got closer to the Flahertys', Rachel loomed out of the darkness, tall and thin, her dark hair flowing down her back, her white nightgown fluttering in the shadows, following the others.

"Rachel!" I said.

Rachel turned her head, as if she'd heard a voice from far away, but she didn't look at me and she didn't stop. She just moved steadily on.

As I was coming up the Flahertys' front walk, their front door flew open and Mrs. Flaherty came out in a state of agitation, her bathrobe flapping around her ankles. "You too?" she exclaimed when she saw me. "Where did Rachel go? Did you see her? Why are you out at night? Why are all these children walking at night? Has everyone gone totally insane? Quick, come inside. I'm going to wake up Henry. We'll try to chase her, I guess. Look—there goes another one."

The other Flahertys were roused by now. Mr. Flaherty was holding Marshall around the waist, and Marshall was silently struggling to free himself. Tim came stumbling downstairs, his hair sticking up in a rooster's comb. "What are you doing here?" he asked me. His parents were shouting directions to each other.

"Can you drive me someplace?" I asked in a low voice.

"Can I what?" I couldn't blame him for sounding surprised.

Mrs. Flaherty appeared with a trench coat tied over her nightclothes and sneakers on her bare feet. "Zoe, call your parents. They'll be wild. I knew we should have taken more drastic action at school! Tim, you stay with Marshall. Hold on to him! He's trying to follow the others up the street. Holler up to your brother and tell him to take the other car and follow us!" Then she raced out the door. Tim lifted Marshall up, saying, "Hey, what's going on, fella?" and held him firmly. Mr. Flaherty rushed after his wife, pulling a sweater over his head as he went. I heard them start their van, parked in front of the house, and they pulled away.

"I've got to stay here," Tim said around Marshall's squirming arms and legs.

"Never mind," I said.

I ran out their front door and started back in the direction I'd come. It was probably a couple of miles from there to Norton's house, and I thought I could run at least half of it if I tried.

It took me only twenty minutes, but I was really out of breath when I got to Norton's. As I ran along, I had been trying to figure out how to wake him but not his mother. I didn't need to, though. He was looking out the screen of his bedroom window, and he came down as soon as he saw me.

"Norton, can you drive your car?"

He stared at me. "I guess so. I mean, yes. My mom doesn't know it, but Uncle Arthur gave me a few lessons."

In a moment he had found the car keys on the hook by their back door. Norton's mother's car was an ancient green Plymouth with rust spots and holes worn in the upholstery. At least it had automatic transmission. I waited by the garage while Norton backed it out. He meant to ease it from its place, but it accidentally shot out onto the driveway. I closed the garage door and jumped in. The car backfired once, and Norton backed on down the driveway. Not bad for an eighth grader. He made a wide arc onto the street, narrowly missing two cars parked on the other side. Then he turned on the headlights and drove smoothly to the intersection and took a right onto Main Street. There were no other cars moving.

"There's a cut-over onto the expressway up here somewhere," he said. He rolled down the window, swerving slightly, and rested his elbow on the door frame. As we went along, we kept seeing children walking alone up the sidewalks and streets. Norton accelerated up the curving ramp and shot onto the highway. Thank goodness no other cars were coming. I let out a deep breath as we settled into our lane. The next thing I knew, we had pulled awfully close to a pickup truck ahead of us. Norton let up on the gas pedal, and the car dragged back. "We didn't come out here when we practiced driving," he muttered.

The turnoff to Chester Hills came up in a few minutes. Norton put on his blinker and moved unsteadily across the highway. Then we were off the highway and onto Route 20, and moments later Norton found the turnoff and the chain beside the PRIVATE sign. He pulled off the road, braked abruptly, and the motor died. The car bucked a couple of times, then shuddered to silence. I slid out and took a deep breath. Insects were singing in the underbrush, but otherwise it was quiet all around. The sky was as light as when the moon is full. I looked around and saw the battered rear end of a station wagon almost buried in the bushes growing over a ditch. I pushed through the branches. A familiar ancient station wagon. I looked through a side window. No one was in it, but the photograph of Mr. O'Hara's daughter was lying loose on the floor in front.

"He has to be here," I said to Norton. "Either he came himself or he was forced."

"You still want to go up?"

I nodded. Far down the paved road behind us, in the distance, I could see a small form trudging upward in the dark. We stepped over the chain and started climbing. We were going pretty fast, and Norton got tired after only a few yards. "I can't get my breath," he said. "Wait up."

I felt very odd, completely awake, filled with energy, and almost weightless. I looked back and saw Norton sit down on a log, breathing heavily and shaking as if he'd been struck sick. Far behind him, at the foot of the hill, a small, pale form appeared, marching up through the shadows.

"Take my hand. You've got to be up there, too," I said.

But he couldn't budge. I could see him clearly in the bright moonlight. "You better tag me here, Zoe, because I'm not sure I can get all the way up," he said. "This is all old school property, you know, so the tag counts."

"Okay." I closed my hand around his wrist. "I've got you." He reached into his pocket and pulled out the few cards he had captured and gave them to me. Christina's was on top.

"I'm going on up," I said. "Try to make it. I don't want to be up there all by myself with her."

"I'll try."

I was in the woods now, and the track narrowed. The long arm of a shrub snagged my hair. I came around a curve and found the FERN RIDGE SCHOOL sign. I took the track to the right and followed it to the top. A child in a white T-shirt was already crawling up the cyclone fence. Through the diamond spaces I could see small figures making their way across the grass, not toward the school, but toward the raised open space where Norton's uncle had set up his telescope.

The moon was full and so bright, I could have read a book by it, yet everything was drained of color. I climbed the fence, crossed the field, and approached the main building.

I heard someone laugh—a light, tantalizing laugh.

"Who's there?" I said. The laugh seemed to come

from outside the school. I saw a hint of silver and then a sickening flash of brilliant sparks. I blinked and looked away, looked at the ground, pressed my fingers to my eyes.

I heard the mocking laugh again, floating as lightly as a Christmas bell.

"Where are you?" I began to see through the purple afterimages. There, at the far end of the main building, silver hair gleamed. Christina stepped around the corner and stood, feet apart, fists on her hips, challenging me.

"He's in here," Christina said.

I walked slowly across the gravel. Out of the corner of my eye I saw children as weightless as ghosts crossing the clearing, singly and in groups, silent, covering the last few yards to the circle of ground that was the highest point of the mountain. I kept myself tense and ready to run if Christina came toward me.

Christina stood well back, out of my reach, and pointed to the door to the building. "He got this far the other day," she said. "Go on, look."

I pulled the door open and looked into the hallway where Norton and I had explored the other night. A man lay facedown, his body concealed beneath a dark overcoat. It had to be Mr. O'Hara. I thought I saw the back of the coat move ever so slightly, as if he had taken a shallow breath.

"Is he alive?" I asked.

Christina shrugged. "I have no idea."

The sky was getting brighter, as if the moon had grown or some sort of light was being shed onto the mountaintop from a height.

"Is this what you did to him?" I asked. "Or those children you captured, did they do it?"

"They didn't have the capacity to kill him. This happened when he forced his way to the top of the mountain, sheer willpower, past the barriers, like the one that stopped Norton. Norton will never make it up here—unless he's captured, that is—and neither will the parents struggling to get to their precious little ones."

"What barriers?" I asked. "I climbed up all right."

"Force-field barriers. Of course you were allowed through, so the game can end. The Transport empowers the barriers. They're so we can lift off with all the children and no messy delays, like the parents trying to grab them back. The Transport began approaching last week, when it became clear the game would be played to its finish." Christina glanced upward, and I saw that the enlarged moon was in fact something else, much larger and closer, descending rapidly over the raised circle in the meadow and shedding a soft but brilliant light.

"Why was he trying to get up here?" I asked.

"What he wanted was to find his daughter. She became a Master Player after she won the game at her school. Mr. O'Hara recognized me as a Master Player when I first came to Oak Hill. I didn't know about him, though, or about his daughter until he told you."

"What's a Master Player?" I asked.

"Someone who wins a complete game, a game that has one of us playing in it. The winner is taken away in the Transport and sent to a colony school. You have to learn what you are told to, and they keep after you until you've learned it. You aren't allowed to flunk. You learn how to adopt any form that could lead to playing a game. That's what I did with you. I watched you at night to see what I should look like. You looked so long at that booklet with the pictures that I decided to use it as a model. I didn't just look at the picture, but at how you thought about it. With us, when we first enter a game, everything is derivative. The last thing we develop is our own minds, and then when the game starts, we're complete, and we can carry through our job as players."

I looked down at the thin stack of cards I was holding. Christina's was on top.

"Now if you tag me," she said, "you'll become a

Master Player. You'll take all these shells of children away in the Transport, and you'll be taught the powers of changing shape and form."

I pictured Dan Fields, white as chalk, plodding up the street in his striped pajamas; Henry Semp, his face expressionless, a single tear running down his cheek as he walked along the sidewalk; even the Duckies, drained of their interesting malice, gray, dry husks, following each other in perfect step. Even if none of them ever was nice to me, I didn't want to take them away to nothingness. What happened to the captured children, all the ones who weren't the winner?

"Or you can give me back my card," said Christina, her voice delicate as silk. "Give it to me and I will release you. All of you."

"What?" I wondered if I was so scared, I had made that up.

"I will release you. The winner doesn't have to bring along the children. They are what fuel the game, are what the game wants, is perpetually greedy for. They are sent out, each one alone, to different parts of the universe to start the game. But the winner can leave them behind."

"Why would you do that?"

"It's always the same—you take the children and then you have to deal with their sickening loneliness and their scruples, and they always want to come home. No matter how hard you try to erase the memory fragment, you can never get it all."

I was pressing the card against my palm, digging my fingers into my flesh to make sure I didn't hand it over under Christina's spell. Something didn't sound right. She had to be trying to trick me. She couldn't want to be captured. Surely there was some punishment for failing to win the game.

"So if I capture you, I win—I go off to be a Master Player," I said. "But if I give you back your card, you'll set us all free."

"Yes, yes." She nodded.

I couldn't imagine being fast enough to outgrab her if I tried to take her by surprise.

"How do I know you can capture me anyhow?" I said. "Show me my card."

She pulled out her bundle of cards. In the brightening light, I could see the one on top. It had my name on it all right, but it wasn't my handwriting. It wasn't the card I had put into the drawing. So would it work or not? Did she know it wasn't my real card?

A tiny prick of light flashed just outside the corner of my eye.

"What was that?" I turned my head and saw a line of pinprick lights moving along the hall, com-

ing from the room where I'd seen the jarful of cocoons.

"You have only a few seconds to decide!" Christina said.

"What are those?"

"Give it! You know you don't want to win the
game! All right, then, never mind, I'll take you!" She
grabbed my wrist and shrilled, "I've got you!"

I stood there with my eyes locked on her pale
hand as it gripped my wrist, and I waited. I waited to
go into a frozen trance, and then, as the seconds
passed, I realized I wasn't changing. I was staying
myself. Our eyes met. Hers were growing larger, and
her face twisted. A silvery sheen began to come over
her skin. "I've got you!" she repeated. "I've got you!
You!"

I yanked my hand away and grabbed her arm.
"I've got *you!*" I said.

"There can't be a trick! There can't be! No trick! I
know everything!" Her voice kept getting higher,
going from squealing to whining and buzzing, like
an angry wasp's. Then it seemed to close itself off. I
squeezed harder, and her makeshift bones crunched
like paper. She fell to the floor. The line of lights
swarmed toward her with a hissing noise, and then
they covered her.

Now light was illuminating everything outside the building. I turned and saw the Transport hovering over the meadow and the field full of Oak Hill children, white as bones, bathed in light, their night-shirts and pajamas fluttering against their fragile bodies, all of them looking in my direction. But they weren't looking at me. Behind me, Mr. O'Hara had pushed himself to his feet. Propping himself up with one hand against the wall, he reached into his coat pocket and pulled out the card I had written with my own hand. He closed his fingers on my shoulder and said, "I win."

The swarm of lights swirled into a tornado shape and streamed past me out toward the alien Transport. Christina was gone. The flooding, pulsing light from the Transport was causing something like a noise, but high-pitched, so I didn't hear it as much as feel it. It was beginning to draw me to it. I could tell I was being compelled toward the ship; I was beginning to want to go; my friends and I would all go together—I could hear their thoughts, a chaos of dwindling wishes to go home, to eat something, to find their mothers before it was too late.

I know Mr. O'Hara squeezed my hand, and he must have released us all with his new powers as a Master Player. I saw him stride across the meadow to the Transport and be taken in by it, alone. The thing gave off even more brilliant light, so I could only look through my fingers, and I saw it leave—a ludicrous, turnip shape now, turning and pulsing above the children, and then it flattened itself like a piece of paper, then curled up to a single line of blinding white light, then shrank to a dot, and then it was gone.

CHAPTER SIXTEEN

Children in nightclothes swarmed everywhere, searching for their parents in the crowd that now surged up the mountain. The little ones were crying, and the older ones, once they got over being embarrassed at being seen in what they wore to bed, were standing around cracking jokes.

"What's this, now—some new kind of school sleep-over?" asked a fireman, who had also been summoned to the scene. Great scorch marks scarred the meadow, visible even by starlight, and a smell of burning grass hung in the air.

"Ugh! How did we ever end up in this foul place?" Claire huddled with the other Duckies on the edge of the field, all of them shivering and hugging themselves, dressed in their fathers' pajama tops.

"How will we ever...," said Elizabeth.

"It's just too...," agreed Kiki.

"Rachel!" Mr. Flaherty shouted as he caught sight of his daughter. Amy was standing beside her, and the three of them wrapped their arms around each other.

"Zoe?" Norton stood a little distance away from me.

"She's gone, Norton. Whatever was in that jar—those sparks—ate her up or something and took her with them. Mr. O'Hara was up here, only just about half-alive, because of the force field or whatever it was—that space thing sent it down to keep everybody off the mountain. But he managed to live long enough to tag me, and I'd already tagged Christina.

"That card the kids took from him in the parking lot? It was a fake too. You know that day we wrote our names on the cards? Before the drawing, he took my real card out and hid it somewhere in the classroom. Then he put a fake card into the stack with his daughter's name on it. Then he wrote *another* fake card with my name on it and let them take it away from him. That way, Christina would be off her guard. So he won, and now he's gone."

"But how did he get to be a player? He wasn't in the drawing."

"Well, in a weird way, it was my card he drew. I guess that counted."

"If you hadn't tagged Christina, well, if Mr. O'Hara hadn't tagged you, we'd all be out there, wouldn't we—somewhere? We'd just end up, well, in *The Chronicle*."

I nodded. Now here came all the rest of the Flahertys, and then my own father, who gave me a hug. And then all of us—Flahertys, Dad, Norton, Amy, and I—had a huge bear hug together.

The fire department and the police were doing their best to get people to leave. "Norton, do you want a ride?" my father asked.

"That's okay, Mr. Brook. I've got the car," said Norton.

My dad looked surprised at that, but it wasn't much compared with other events. We three walked down the mountain road together. At the bottom, I caught sight of Mr. O'Hara's station wagon again. I pressed through the bushes, opened the passenger door a crack, and reached in for the photograph and the frame. I couldn't figure out why he'd taken out the picture and left it behind. It didn't seem right to leave it here in the abandoned car.

"What do you have there?" my dad asked. "Whose car is this?"

"My teacher's," I said. "I'm going to keep this for him."

"Well, where is he? Looks like everybody else from school is here. Isn't he coming back for his car? Is he up there with the others?"

"No. He left town after that attack, Dad. His car—maybe it broke down here."

My father frowned at the unlikeliness of that tale, but I knew he was not disposed to argue tonight.

"So what is the picture?" he asked me.

"It's his daughter," I said. I tried to pat the pieces of the frame and cardboard backing together. And then the notion whisked through my head that this could be a good place to hide something, something small and flat, like half an index card.

My father had turned away. "I'll follow you home," he said to Norton. "Just to make sure everybody gets where they're supposed to go."

Oak Hill School was entirely back to normal by the time of our eighth-grade graduation. The matter of the children all leaving their homes in the middle of the night and walking to Chickatawbut Hill was discussed for a while but never completely explained. People of good sense concluded that it was best to call the whole thing an episode of brain fever, or to say that some irresponsible nature freak had led them all up there, and that the numbers were exaggerated in any case—it couldn't possibly have been the whole school.

Elimination was never again played at Oak Hill School.

However, a couple of years later, I heard that Josh Perkins had been sitting with his cousin on the beach in North Carolina one summer's day, and he began to tell him about the crazy game that his school used to play. The cousin was interested. He listened to the whole story and asked about the rules. He said he might see if his school would like to try it in the fall.

On the evening of graduation, I stood in my room, nearly ready to leave for the ceremony, looking out the window into my backyard. I had tried a bottle of hair stuff that Amy said Claire said was great, and it actually worked, sort of—my hair shone in the mirror, and the usual fringe of curls and kinks had at least spread itself out evenly across the top of my head. My dress was new and still smelled new—crisp white cotton with satin piping and tiny satin buttons that pleased my mother. I saw that it fit my long waist exactly and that my arms looked graceful in the short sleeves. *Graceful?* Was it possible? Was it even desirable? I choked back a laugh. Things weren't turning out so badly.

Tim had promised me he was going to tell me everything I needed to know about being a freshman next year, and meantime he might take me out for a driving lesson once he got his license this summer.

Norton had come over in the afternoon to help me put up decorations outside for the party. My mother had come up with all sorts of objections to having a party, but my father had not, and I just went ahead and invited everybody. Norton and I blew up balloons and arranged chairs and bug candles and strung Christmas lights in the apple trees and figured out where to put the stereo speakers. Afterward we sat on the floor in my room and drank Cokes and Norton told me about a chess tournament he was thinking of going to. I did feel the tiniest tweak of dismay—a chess tournament? What kind of guys go to those? I'd been sitting there imagining him growing ten inches and playing soccer. We stayed silent for a while, and then Norton leaned over and—I knew it was coming—kissed me. His breath came gently across my face, and I tasted his tongue, which I was not sure I wanted to, and then he kind of reached his hand across to hold my side and incidentally part of my breast, so I sat there, growing warm. Then he drew back, took his hand away, and said, "Just this once, Zoe."

I gave him a shaky little smile, during which my lip somehow got snagged on a front tooth, and I said, "That's all right."

"Zoe?" My mother called up the stairs. "Are you ready?"

"Sure."

We had to park up the street from the school, and then the three of us walked down the hill together. There was Norton with his mother and his uncle Arthur. Girls in white dresses and boys in unaccustomed coats and ties were collecting in the June twilight, while their mothers passed slowly into the flower-filled hall, dabbing their eyes with tissues, and their fathers genially hailed other fathers.

As the class lined up outside for the procession, I craned my neck to look for the few stars beginning to sparkle in the blue dusk, and I sent up a quick wish that, wherever in the universe Mr. O'Hara and his daughter were, they had found each other. The string quartet, nearly in tune, began to play, and the line stepped forward.

8402